About the Author

Author photo by Marzena Pogorzaly

Hugh Canham has had two fulfilling careers: his first was as a solicitor with a central London law firm, where he became Managing Partner and briefly Chairman, during a period of great expansion when the firm had offices in Hong Kong, Los Angeles and Singapore. In the 1980s he switched his attentions to running a small farm in East Sussex and an antiques shop and gallery in Cranbrook in Kent with his wife. Hugh is the author of two novels published by Book Guild Publishing. He now lives in London.

By the same author

The New Leaf, Book Guild Publishing 2014
Lucasta & Hector, Book Guild Publishing 2015

GOING AWAY

and other stories

Hugh Canham

To Caroline

Love,

Hugh.

Book Guild Publishing
Sussex, England

First published in Great Britain in 2015 by
The Book Guild Ltd
The Werks
45 Church Road
Hove, BN3 2BE

The stories 'In the Course of Duty', 'Going Away', 'Swan Song', 'The Recompense' and 'Salvation' were all first published in *Quadrant* magazine in Australia

Typesetting in Baskerville by
Ellipsis Digital Ltd, Glasgow

Printed and bound in Great Britain by
CPI Group (UK) Ltd, Croydon, CR0 4YY

A catalogue record for this book is available from
The British Library.

ISBN 978 1 910298 79 4

To the memory of my wife Sheena 1936–2011
and our son Hamish 1962–2003

Contents

In the Course of Duty

Police Constable Kevin Long crouched low in the bushes beside the bend in the road. He was beginning to sweat profusely and flies buzzed around his head. His knees ached. He was having great difficulty operating the speed gun he had been told to use.

'Look, lad,' the Sergeant had said, 'this morning I want you to go to the Staples Row crossroads. You know where I mean. There's a sharp bend in the B85 to the north before the crossroads. Four or five notices telling people to slow down to thirty both beside and on the road, but nobody takes a blind bit of notice! Been three accidents in the last month. I want you to take this contraption and catch a few speeders. It'll get written up in the local press and make people more careful! I'll show you how to use it. It's easy – even you should get the hang of it quite quickly!'

And so the Sergeant had ferried PC Long out to the crossroads along with the speed gun and told him he wanted at least four people caught by lunchtime.

'Keep down as much as possible, lad . . . if they see you they'll brake hard.'

Well, it wasn't that easy. Because it was a very sharp bend you didn't have any time at all to point the machine at the car before it whizzed past. PC Long decided that if he was going to get a good shot of any approaching car on the other side of the road (which was his objective), he'd have to listen for it coming and then at the last minute squirm onto the road itself. But he must take his jersey off first. Of course, just as he was taking it off he missed a wonderful opportunity – sports car, must have been doing sixty, nearly on two wheels as it went round the bend. Well, he would definitely get the next one. It was already eleven thirty!

He was tensed up when he heard the next car coming. Yes, it sounded like a fast one. He moved into the road in a crouching position and was about to point the gun when he suddenly felt a terrible thud on his protruding backside and a female voice shouted, 'Shit . . .' Then he was lying face downwards on the road. When he looked up, dazed, the speed gun was lying several yards up the road broken into two pieces. Beyond that was a racing bicycle on its side with its wheel still spinning, and beyond that, in the bushes, the spread-eagled figure of a young woman in shorts.

PC Long heaved himself up and staggered towards the girl. Even in his dazed state he noticed she was very pretty with lovely long brown legs. She reminded him of one of the pictures in the magazine he'd been looking at in bed the previous night before his mother had banged on his door and told him to stop reading and turn his light off otherwise he'd be late for the early shift. The girl seemed to be bleeding from the head. He experimentally tapped her cheek. She seemed unconscious. Then he patted one of her thighs. Yes, she was definitely out. She must have hit her head pretty hard. Bugger! It was his fault, he supposed, but he was only trying to do his job. Well, now he'd better take some action. He remembered his first aid. He mustn't try and move her. Call an ambulance! . . . No, call the

Sergeant first and tell him what had happened. He might want to attend the incident himself.

At about the same time, Darren Collins, Chief Negotiator for Percy & Co., Estate Agents, had just risen from a double bed in the end-of-terrace council house where he had been making love to Tiffany Cross. Tiffany had managed to secure the council house and have her rent subsidised because she was a single mother. Her 13-month-old daughter, Wanda, was asleep in the next bedroom.

'Do you have to go just yet, Darren?' Tiffany pleaded, propping herself up in bed on one elbow.

'Sorry love, got to show an old bird round the Manor. Very important sale for us. If I don't hurry I'll be late.'

'Oh Darren, when are you going to come to me, perm?'

Oh Lord, she's off again, thought Darren.

'You said you would, you know. You promised, that time!'

'Look, it's not that easy.' Thank God she hadn't started on about it before they'd got into bed. It would have had an adverse effect on his erectile tissues.

'I can't stop now, darling. Must go.'

He quickly buttoned up his shirt, put his tie round his shoulders and slipped out of the door, forgetting his jacket, which was still on the back of a chair.

'Bugger him,' said Tiffany, hitting the pillow on which Darren's head had been recently resting. 'I'll go and see that wife of his if he's not careful!'

Darren didn't stop to tie his tie as he got into his car. He'd have a little bit of time to spare later. The thing was to get away from the house quickly before Tiffany came running down the garden path in the nude and crying, or something silly like that. After he'd put half a mile or so between himself and the council houses he slowed down, stopped, twisted the driving mirror round and tied his tie. He'd pulled up in front of three newly built houses. 'Executive homes' you'd call them. Very nice if you could afford one! The front gardens were still being landscaped and there was a pile of top soil by one of the gateways. Three sparrows were having a dust bath in the sunshine. Darren watched them, fascinated. They made him feel somewhat sad. Although they were obviously enjoying themselves, they quarrelled and attacked one another from time to time.

After he'd shown the client round the Manor he'd got to go and pick up his small son, Barry, from school at lunchtime. The school had the afternoon off for some reason – he couldn't remember what, but as his wife, Doreen, worked every day until three o'clock he said he'd do it and look after Barry until she came home. He thought of Barry and how he always ran towards his dad and clasped him round the knees whenever he saw him. How could he leave Barry and go to live with Tiff, even though he liked her much more than Doreen at the moment? All Doreen wanted to do these days was go on holidays and buy more things for the house.

He looked at his watch. God! He was going to be late for his appointment to view the Manor unless he drove like fury. He'd been sitting looking at those stupid sparrows for much longer than he'd thought.

He was probably doing fifty miles per hour when he rounded the bend before the Staples Row crossroads. The Sergeant had just stopped and parked his car as far off the road as the hedge would allow, opposite where PC Long was bending over the cyclist. Although the Sergeant had put his hazard warning lights on, Darren was going so fast that he only saw them at the last moment. He clipped the offside rear of the police car hard from behind, slewed round in the road and overturned.

'Oh my God!' yelled the Sergeant as smoke began to erupt from the radiator of the upturned car. 'Quick, let's try to get him out, lad, before the bloody thing goes up in flames!'

Somehow they got Darren out. They noticed that the front air bag had failed to open and he wasn't wearing his seat belt. Between them they carried him away from the car just before it exploded. He looked in a pretty bad way.

Although an ambulance had arrived to deal with the cyclist, another one was now also called to carry Darren off to the Accident & Emergency Department of the local hospital. When the two accident victims were received there, it was noted that neither of them had been carrying any identification.

Because Darren didn't turn up to fetch Barry from school, his mum, Doreen, was phoned at work and was asked to collect him. She was very worried. She couldn't understand where Darren had got to. He didn't answer his mobile, which he always carried in his car. She phoned his estate agency. They were worried too. He hadn't turned up to show the lady round the Manor and the lady was very cross.

By two o'clock, Tiffany had made a decision. She'd had two gins with the fish and chips from the van that always called round on a Thursday. As Darren hadn't come back for his jacket, she was going to take it back to his house and talk to his wife. She knew exactly where Darren lived. It was quite a walk, but never mind. She put on a bit of makeup, strapped Wanda in her pram and set out purposefully with Darren's jacket draped over the handle.

Meanwhile, the Sergeant had made a preliminary report to the station about the incidents and summoned photographers and the forensics people. He'd organised a breakdown lorry to remove the burnt-out wreck of Darren's car. As he drove his badly dented car back to the station with a glum PC Long beside him, he started to have forebodings about what the Superintendent was going to say to both of them!

At the campsite, Michael had been sitting in the sun by the camper van getting steadily crosser and crosser. It was the third time during their holiday that Sandra had ridden off on her bike in a tantrum. She'd come back after about an hour the last two times, but this time she'd been gone over three hours! They were supposed to pack up and go home that afternoon as he had to be at work the next day. It was, he thought savagely, time to put an end to it all. They lived in his house. He earned all the money, paid all the bills and the mortgage. She just sat around all day writing this novel which she would never let him read and seemingly never progressed further than the first three chapters – which she kept on rewriting . . . She could, of course, have cycled the whole way home – it was only about forty miles – or she could have had an accident! Both unlikely. Sod it, he would pack up. He loaded his own racing bike onto the back of the camper van and drove off angrily. By the time he reached the motorway he'd definitely decided to get rid of Sandra. There was that rather nice girl at work who kept smiling at him!

*

'Daddy will be home soon, I expect,' said Doreen to Barry, who was sitting at the kitchen table colouring a book which she'd bought him on the way home from school to make up for the disappointment that Dad hadn't collected him as promised. 'I can't think what's become of him.'

There was a ring at the front door bell. She went and opened it. It was a small, dark young girl who she'd never seen before with a baby in a pram.

'I've come to bring Darren's jacket back. He left it behind,' announced the girl, waving Darren's jacket in the air.

'Oh,' said Doreen. She immediately thought that Darren must have been looking round the girl's house to value it or something like that. 'Thank you. Would you like to come in for a moment and bring the baby? You see, I'm worried about Darren, he seems to have disappeared.'

The girl turned her head sharply as she started unstrapping the baby.

'How do you mean, disappeared?'

'Well, he was supposed to pick up young Barry from school, dinner time, but he didn't turn up. I've rung the office but they haven't heard from him either. He didn't turn up to show a lady round the Manor. When did he leave you?'

Tiffany had a sudden strange feeling that this wife must know all about her and Darren.

'Suppose it must have been about eleven-thirty-ish,' she said defiantly.

'You'd better come through into the lounge,' said Doreen. 'Barry's in the kitchen. I don't want him worried.'

This girl looked a bit like a gypsy. Surely she couldn't be selling a house?

'Have you phoned the police or the hospital?' she asked.

'No, not yet,' replied Doreen.

'Mum, who's that?' shouted Barry from the kitchen.

'Oh, just a lady who's called,' Doreen shouted. Then to Tiffany, 'Look, dear, I don't know your name.'

'Tiffany, but people call me Tiff.'

'Well, Tiffany, I think you're right. Would you please go and talk to Barry in the kitchen and keep him there while I phone? I don't want him listening.'

Tiffany picked up her baby and walked slowly into the kitchen to see Barry. God – he looked so like Darren as he turned and looked at her.

'This is Wanda, Barry. I brought her in to see you.'

She put Wanda on the floor and Barry watched fascinated as Wanda crawled towards him using her elbows and knees.

A few minutes later Doreen put her head round the door and anxiously beckoned to Tiffany. She whispered, 'The hospital say that they've got an accident case, man and a woman, neither with any identification. Both unconscious. They think I'd better go and see if it's Darren. About the right age, apparently. Early thirties. It's only five minutes' walk to the hospital. If I phone my mum it'll take her about an hour to get here. Could you possibly hang on a bit and look after Barry? I'll be back as soon as possible.'

'Sure,' said Tiffany. 'We're all getting on fine!'

She went and sat back at the kitchen table and helped Barry with his colouring book. Wanda carried on crawling round the floor and eventually came to Barry's chair and hauled herself up onto her feet and stood swaying and looking up at him for about thirty seconds until she fell backwards onto her padded bottom and laughed. Barry laughed too.

'Do it again, Wanda,' he said.

'I don't think she understands you,' said Tiffany. She was trying to stay calm and bright but all the time she was worried. God, she hoped that it wasn't Darren unconscious in hospital.

'Where's Mum?' asked Barry suddenly.

'Oh, she's just popped out for a few minutes. She'll be back soon.'

'I want my tea.'

'Well, you'll just have to wait a bit.'

Barry turned and looked up at her. 'Well can I have a drink of orange then please?'

Darren and Sandra were lying side by side on trolleys in the assessment room.

'Yes, that's my Darren,' said Doreen.

'Do you know this young lady at all?'

Doreen looked at Sandra and shook her head. How had Darren ended up in this accident with this blonde girl? The girl had a terrible injury to her head, but Darren looked awful – much worse. The nurse gave Doreen a chair and took some particulars and a bit later a young doctor came and sat beside her and spoke to her. She only vaguely took in what he was saying.

Skull fractured . . . would have to operate. Possible injury to the spine and broken arms . . . Difficult to say what the results would be . . . As she lived so near and had a small son to look after, no point in waiting . . . Best to go home – they'd phone.

Tiffany could tell immediately that things were bad when she saw Doreen's face as she came into the kitchen.

'Barry, you just look after Wanda a minute would you?' she said to Doreen's son. 'I just want to have a word with your mum.'

They went into the lounge.

'Yes, it's Darren,' Doreen confirmed. 'He's been in an accident with some young girl. I've never seen her before. Both unconscious. He's got a fractured skull and maybe injuries to his back. They're going to have to operate.' Doreen sat down in an armchair and began to cry. It was funny, but she noticed Tiffany was crying as well.

'I'm very sorry,' Tiffany said. 'I'd better go now. Barry said he wants his tea. I gave him some orange squash.'

She went and fetched Wanda. *Who the hell was the blonde girl he was with?* she wondered.

'Look, this is my phone number,' she said as she went into the lounge again on her way out, and pushed a piece of paper into Doreen's hand. 'Let me know what happens.'

Doreen couldn't seem to move from the armchair. She crumpled the piece of paper and let it drop on the floor. Two minutes later she looked at it and wondered where it had come from.

A little later Barry came through from the kitchen and stood and looked at his mother.

'I heard you crying . . . Why are you crying, Mum?' he asked. 'Is it something to do with that lady?'

The Sergeant was called in to see the Superintendent.

'You've heard that the motorist has died and the cyclist is on the critical list?'

The Sergeant nodded.

'Potentially we have two actions against this police force. It's a serious matter, Bill. Why on earth did you send young Kevin out with a speed gun and leave him unsupervised?'

'I didn't know what else to do with him, sir. He's not very good at anything.'

'My very point, Bill! And then why on earth did you park your car on a blind corner?'

'It was in the course of duty, sir. I was rushing to the scene of an incident. I parked tight up against the hedge and put the hazard warning lights on!'

The Superintendent sighed. Like many in positions of authority before him he could see himself taking the blame for all this even though he'd had nothing directly to do with it.

Just before he went home for the evening, PC Kevin Long heard the terrible news that the cyclist had also died in hospital. He simply couldn't believe it. He hadn't thought that she was that seriously injured!

When he got home, his mother thought he was very quiet. Eventually she asked him what the matter was.

'Woman cyclist hit me while I was doing a speed-gun trap. She fell off and died later in hospital.'

'Oh,' said his Mum. 'Well, not your fault!'

'Suppose not. Just happened!'

While his mother was washing up, he went quietly up to his bedroom and found the girly magazine he'd been looking at the previous night. He put it into an old plastic carrier bag and then crept down the stairs and out into the back yard. He stuffed it right down into the bottom of the rubbish bin and put the lid back on the bin. He then stood for several minutes as the darkness was falling with his eyes closed.

Going Away

The taxi fare from his flat to the Club was always about five bob. It seemed to stay at that for years. And then with metrication (or was it decimalisation?) it started to creep up and up and then it was about five pounds. He had started taking the tube a long time ago: much cheaper. And for ages now, it had cost him nothing at all as he had his pensioner's travel pass. And the subscription to the Club had gone down too, as he was over 75 and had been a member for such a long time. Just as well, too, with interest rates being so low and the stock market at rock bottom, seemingly for ever!

The walk through St James's Park from the Underground station to The Mall was really most pleasant. He always stopped on the bridge over the lake and looked first to the left at the fountains and the Palace, and then to the right. And when he turned to the right he always thought of Churchill and the war. And now there was that funny wheel thing in the sky, called for some reason 'The Eye'. Quite nice, really. But in the spring and in the summer, as it now was, there were all these tourists messing up the park. Hardly another English person to be seen. And smelly hot dog stalls, even though there was a big notice saying they were unauthorised and you were likely to get food poisoning from them. Funny that people still ate from them. It was because none of them could read English, he supposed.

And their dress was appalling. For instance, baseball caps worn back to front, funny T-shirts and flappy shorts below the knee for the men. And all the females had on either jeans or tight black trousers.

One had to keep up appearances in spite of what the rest of the world was doing. In the old days he'd always worn a bowler hat, of course, and when they went out of fashion, a trilby; never a panama, not to the Club. And the only concession for a heat wave, as was now the case, was to leave off the waistcoat. And a rolled umbrella always.

An Indian girl in a very low-cut top and the usual tight black trousers rushed across his path laughing and giggling with two small Indian children. For a moment he was reminded of his divorce those long years ago. He'd been so stupid to fight it; but it had seemed so unfair. Accused of cruelty. In those days, everything had to come out in open court and he'd been terrified; but after the barrister had said to the judge, 'There is, I'm afraid, some bad sexual evidence here, m'lud,' he'd then fortunately continued, 'Perhaps I could hand it up to you rather than read it out in open court? I gather that part of the evidence is not contested.' Even though there'd not been much about it in the papers, he'd felt for years that people in the Bank had looked at him strangely. Nowadays! – well, it would have been quite different. Nobody would care. And after Marion's departure and her money no longer available, it had been a sad do. But there was the MBE for his charitable work. The medal stood in its open case in the china cabinet in his flat.

An interminable wait at the traffic lights in The Mall and then up to the Marlborough Gate and into St James's Street. Goodness, it was hot. He mopped his brow discreetly as he deposited his hat and umbrella in the cloakroom, and then again in the bar as the barman poured him his usual dry sherry.

'Be closed in another week. Where are you going away to?' the other man at the bar enquired.

He had forgotten that the Club would be closed for an entire month so soon.

'Don't know yet. Have to get out of London for August, I suppose. Even more foreigners then than there are now, and that's saying something!'

'Dead right, old chap. Terrible, isn't it? Not what we fought the war for. Invaded by everyone now!'

'Too true.'

He hadn't really thought of it that way before; but old Smithy was right. But he didn't want to go on talking to him for any longer than necessary and looked round hopefully for his friend, John. There he was, just coming into the entrance hall. He waved through the doorway to him and went and sat in an armchair. John would soon come in. But when John came into the bar he had a friend with him.

'See you tomorrow – lunching with my old pal Peter Mills today. He's come up from Brighton specially.'

Ah, well! It would have to be the members' table, then. He ordered his favourite, even though it was a bit heavy for the hot weather – cod's roe followed by steak and kidney pudding, with a small carafe of the Club's claret.

A member he did not know at all came and sat beside him. He seemed quite young, must be a new chap, fifty at most, very dark, black pinstriped suit, black hair.

'Going away soon?' the young man enquired.

'Hope to,' he said. His mind wandered to the hotel he used to stay at in Devon. It had changed ownership two years ago and he hadn't liked to go since. Last August, he'd gone to see his sister, but she had died in the spring.

'I'm off to Tuscany with the family for three weeks. Wonderful! Ever been?'

'Er … no,' he said.

'You should try it!'

'I'd certainly like to get out of London in August with all these tourists here.'

'Bit of a pain, I agree, but good for balance of payments, you know!'

'I suppose so.'

He really must go away, he thought, as an hour later he walked down St James's Street. The heat rose from the pavement into his face. His collar felt very tight and sweat began to trickle down his chest.

In the park the tourists still milled around, it seemed in even greater numbers, and as he walked down the path he was beginning to feel slightly sick and his head was pounding. He came to the bridge and leant on the railings with his head down.

'Are you all right, sir?' a voice was saying.

No, he didn't really think he was. He shook his head.

'Come over here where there's a bit of shade and sit down on the grass, sir, and you will feel better.'

He looked at the man who was leading him gently by the arm. He was Chinese!

'Just sit down, or maybe you would prefer to lie. I will roll my jacket up and put it under your head.'

How very kind, he thought. Yes, he did feel much more

comfortable lying down with his hat off and something under his head.

'I'm a doctor. May I please feel your heart and your pulse?'

'Er, yes, of course. I don't feel too good. Must be the heat. I think you're a sort of Good Samaritan.' But then he thought, silly thing to say – a Chinese chap wouldn't know about the Bible.

He saw the trees and the sky above his head and felt the doctor loosening his collar and saying something about he'd called for an ambulance on his mobile phone. But it didn't really matter; he was going away and it would be all right then. The trees and the sky looked like Devon already. And he was definitely going … going away … Gone.

I Blamed the Oysters

Driving off Le Shuttle at Calais I started to regret what I was doing. It so disturbed me that I almost took the wrong autoroute, the A16 southwards instead of the A26 eastwards. My sudden change of direction prompted a great deal of Gallic hooting and I could hear Jean's voice in my head saying crossly, 'Why on earth don't you get a satnav?' I quickly blocked her voice out and tried to enjoy the views of the French countryside. It was early May and everything looked beautifully fresh and green. But glimpses of lines of crosses marking the war cemeteries reminded me of what I had come to do.

I arrived at the hotel I had been aiming for in Châlons-en-Champagne just in time for dinner. In spite of its wonderful wines, I had never thought much of the countryside of Champagne. But I'd been told that the food at this hotel was excellent and indeed it proved to be and the whole evening cheered me up considerably. The head waiter who took my order spoke almost perfect English so I did not have to struggle with my very limited and rusty French. The dinner proceeded slowly. I had *pâté de foie gras*, a veal dish with a creamy sauce, cheese and a chocolate dessert; very bad, no doubt, for my cholesterol at the age of 45 but meticulously and elegantly served by a beautiful waitress. Well, she seemed beautiful to me; she might not have appealed to everyone. She was short and thin and had long black hair, which kept falling over her small dark face as she leant over to serve, so that she had to keep brushing it back. Why didn't she use a hairclip? I wondered. I suppose because she thought the falling hair made her attractive. As she pushed it back she always smiled at me and from time to time she spoke a word or two of English, such as, 'You're welcome'. But I had the feeling this was all supposed to be a joke between us. At the end of the meal I asked her her name.

'They call me Mimi,' she said and laughed. Was this another joke? I wondered.

Pleasantly fortified by the meal and a large Armagnac afterwards, I lay in bed and thought about Mimi for some time before I went to sleep.

In the morning I awoke with a terrible headache. Whether this was caused by having too much to drink or the anxiety of what lay ahead of me I was not sure. I had hoped to see Mimi at breakfast but she was obviously not on duty, so I consoled myself with three cups of black coffee and a yoghurt. But when I came to pay the bill, my dinner, I noticed, had proved rather expensive!

And so, rather later than I had intended, I set out for my destination; an obscure village somewhere to the south and east of Troyes. I inevitably got lost and had to stop and buy one of those yellow-covered Michelin local maps before I found it. Why didn't I buy a satnav? I suppose because I just like map-reading; although it is difficult when driving on your own.

I assumed the graveyard would be somewhere near the church but I could see no sign of it as I stopped in the village square. An old lady dressed in black was locking the church door, as it was just after midday. She waddled across the square and went into into a small house, slamming the door behind her. I did not feel an enquiry about the whereabouts of the graveyard by knocking on her door would be at all welcome. Several people were, however, disappearing through the doorway of a bar/restaurant on the other side of the square. I could ask in there. It looked a run-down sort of a place from the outside and, even worse as I entered through a small cloud of buzzing flies. It was already crowded. A lady approached me and before I could ask the whereabouts of the cemetery, snapped, 'Pour déjeuner, Monsieur? Ici, s'il vous plaît,' and I was almost pushed down into the third of four chairs at a table covered with a plastic tablecloth at which an elderly French couple were already seated, starting to eat plates of soup. They both gave me a faint smile. A few seconds later a large carafe of red wine and a jug of water were plonked in front of me together with a metal dish of sliced French bread, followed rapidly by a bowl of soup.

Ah well! I hadn't had much breakfast. The soup was delicious. By the time I'd eaten a meat course and some cheese I realised I'd drunk the whole carafe of wine. It was replaced by another. I thought of what I had to do and drank two more glasses. Then all I wanted to do was to go to sleep. I even wondered if they had bedrooms to let upstairs but then a fly alighted on the cheese I was eating and I looked at the plastic tablecloth and the shabby wall coverings and decided against it. So, when the serving lady came and asked me for what seemed a trivial amount in Euros for the meal, I asked the whereabouts of the cemetery. It was apparently about half a kilometre down the lane which led off the left of the square.

As I made my way to the car I wondered if I was fit to drive; but there was not far to go!

The cemetery was on the left-hand side of the lane and surrounded by a low wall. I parked just beyond the cemetery wall on a patch of grass beside a vast field of maize which stretched almost as far as I could see. There was a faint noise from an autoroute in the distance beyond it. Apart from that everything was quiet.

I opened the metal gate which led from the lane through the wall of the cemetery. There was a lady on her knees by the side of the path that led between the graves, arranging flowers on one of them. Where did I start to look? I kept walking down the path but everyone seemed to have died in the last century. Had I come to the wrong place? Then I saw that the end of the path led into a newer bit of the cemetery. Eventually I found it. There was a small headstone inscribed in English, 'Rose. Taken from us aged 5'. No surname, just the date of her death. This was what I had come to see. But all I could feel, no doubt fuelled by the amount of wine I had drunk, was absolute rage. The faint noise of the autoroute in the distance annoyed me still further.

'You miserable bitch!' I shouted at the top of my voice. 'Taken from us? You took her from me, you cow!'

I went and punched the wall of the cemetery in my fury and then licked my grazed and bloody knuckles. I leant against the cemetery wall and thought of Rose, aged maybe 2½, shrieking with laughter as she slid down the back of our sofa and Jean and I laughing too to encourage her to do it again. Rose's chubby little legs were so sweet then and now they were rotting away in that grave over there. I realised I should have bought some flowers, but I hadn't. I went and picked five daisies from a patch of grass and put them on the grave but the wind blew them away almost at once so I had to pick five more and put a stone on top of the stems. Had Jean done the wording deliberately? Probably. She'd done everything to keep me from Rose in life after she'd taken her away and until a week ago had even kept the whereabouts of her grave a secret. I thought bitterly about the email I'd received at my office last December.

'Regret Rose died today. Jean.'

I leant against the cemetery wall, gazed over the field of maize and remembered the day two years ago. For months previously Jean had become more and more critical of me. She said that I ate and drank too much, was indecisive, weak and self-deluding and didn't stand up to other people. Also, I spent too much time running my architectural practice and not enough time with her and Rose. Some of the criticism was undoubtedly true. But I'd always been like that and Jean never seemed to mind when I first knew her and we spent the weekends together. I suppose it's when you live with someone all the time that they start annoying you.

It was Rose's birthday. We were sitting at home in the kitchen having breakfast. It was raining very hard outside. Jean was reminding me yet again that she expected me home early by four o'clock in time for Rose's birthday tea. She was having a few small friends round and there was to be a cake with candles.

'Yes, yes,' I said, 'it's in my diary.'

And then my mobile rang. It was the sort of call that any architect dreads. The office block I had just designed and had built for a very well-known public company was leaking. Not just through the roof but on every one of the eight floors there was water falling like rain through the ceilings. The staff who had arrived early for work had been sent home. Computers, desks and carpets were all going to be ruined. I remember looking at the red and white checked tablecloth and the squares seemed to dance before my eyes.

'I must go,' I said to Jean. 'There's been a disaster at that new office block; water is pouring through all the ceilings.'

Jean gave me what I would call a 'steady' look. It was not at all sympathetic.

'Well, mind you're back in time for Rose's party,' she said.

Unfortunately the office block was thirty miles away from where we lived and it took me two hours to get there as the roads were flooded. When I arrived it was worse than I'd feared.

The Managing Director of the company greeted me with, 'Ah, here you are at last! Frankly, I'll kill whoever is to blame for this. The builder's late too. For God's sake sort it out between you!'

I thought – I must be to blame. I had designed the building and supervised the builders. There would probably be a negligence claim against me for millions of pounds! I paced through the building floor by floor with an umbrella over my head and my feet squelching on the soaking carpets while the builder's men removed panels from the false ceilings and swore a great deal.

It turned out in the end that it was no fault of mine. There was a large piece of wood jammed down one of the two downpipes from the roof, causing the rainwater to back up and enter the air conditioning system. Until now there had not been any heavy rains since the building had been finished. The building contractor was very cagey about it but I gathered he had some idea of who might have maliciously dropped the wood into the downpipe. My anxiety had made me forget all about Rose's birthday tea. By the time I remembered and looked at my watch it was four-thirty and of course I was thirty miles away. I should have telephoned but I did not think I could properly explain what had happened and why I had been so anxious by talking to Jean on the phone while she was in the middle of a children's party.

By the time I had driven home I felt relieved but exhausted. The remains of the birthday tea were on the red checked tablecloth in the kitchen with a note propped up against a nearly empty bottle of orange squash.

'You will no doubt not be interested to know that Rose had a very nice birthday tea, following which I have taken her with me to live abroad. Do not bother to try and find out where we are as we do not wish to see you.'

I took one last look at the grave and the five already wilting daisies then sadly I made my way back to the car. My knuckles were still bleeding and I wrapped my handkerchief around them. I thought I had been at Rose's grave for a long time but the lady was still on her knees arranging the flowers on the grave in the old part of the cemetery as I passed her.

When I sat down in the car I felt all I wanted to do was to go back to the hotel in Châlons and see Mimi. What exactly I wanted from her I was not sure. I just had a great desire to see her again.

In due course I sat in the salon fortifying myself with a large whisky before dinner, peering through the archway into the dining room to see if Mimi was there.

'Very nice to see you again, sir,' said the head waiter. 'We have some very good oysters tonight.'

'Yes, that would be nice,' I said. 'Six please. And then the veal dish I had last night. It was very good. By the way is Mimi on duty tonight?'

'Mimi, sir?'

'Yes, your waitress.'

'No sir, she was called Mathilde. She has left.'

'Left! But where has she gone to?'

'I really couldn't say, sir. Yesterday was her last day.' The fellow was so smooth he could have been a waiter in a London club.

I felt very disconsolate. When I started to eat the oysters, surely, I thought, you should only eat oysters when there's an 'r' in the month and this is May! But probably the French don't care about things like that; after all they eat thrush paté!

I was very sick in the night. I blamed the oysters but it wasn't really them, I know. I was sick at heart.

Swan Song

Sitting on the train to Eastbourne, looking at the seemingly interminable and unintelligible graffiti on the buildings beside the line, he wondered if it had really been a good idea, booking himself into this hotel for Christmas. He'd had an impulse, thinking he didn't want to be alone over the holiday, as both his neighbours were going to be away. He and Ethel had spent two summer holidays at the hotel and then one Christmas, five years ago, just before she became ill. A quiet, old-fashioned sort of place.

'Well, you've left it a bit late, sir, but you're in luck!' the receptionist had said when he telephoned. 'We've just had a cancellation. Nice single room, small, but overlooking the sea.'

So he took it. 'Arrive Christmas Eve, leave the day after Boxing Day.' He'd been sent a 'Programme of Events'. 'We hope,' it said, 'that gentlemen will wear their dinner jackets in the evening.'

He'd looked his out, finding it at the back of the wardrobe, and tried it on. He hadn't worn it for five years, since that last Christmas at the hotel. It was so old that it looked a trifle green in places and the jacket was a bit loose. He'd lost weight while looking after Ethel. But it would have to do.

Little seemed to have changed in Eastbourne as he took the taxi from the station – and the hotel was certainly just the same:

even the same hall porter, and the open fire burning in the hall, although it was scarcely necessary as it was so mild.

'Of course I remember you, sir!' the porter said. 'On your own now, are you? I'm sorry!'

The bedroom was very small but quite comfortable, and it had a wonderful view out to sea and over to Beachy Head. He unpacked slowly and put his alarm clock on the bedside table next to the folding photograph frame. One half had a picture of Ethel taken many years ago when she was principal boy in *Cinderella* at the Palladium and the other half showed her some years later in a studio pose with her fine features three-quarters on to the camera, smiling.

It was 3.45 and nearly teatime, but he didn't feel he could face tea in the lounge as he remembered it. There would be strange smiling faces and he wouldn't know what to say without Ethel. She'd always been so good at that sort of thing. So he put on his hat and coat again and went for a walk along the seafront. It was a good day for the time of year but getting dark, of course, and there was a stiff breeze off the sea as he walked slowly towards Beachy Head. He'd always thought it was a strange way of committing suicide, jumping off Beachy Head. If you wanted to do it, why not some pills? But mustn't think about that sort of thing. He'd resolved to keep his pecker up after Ethel passed on.

He and Ethel had had a wonderful life together. They'd met in the theatre at Newcastle-on-Tyne. They were both very young. Ethel was a dancer and singer and he was trying to be a comedian. But he'd never managed to be a very good one. So difficult to make people laugh. And after a time he'd taken to being a manager and agent. Ethel had been really good. She had that special something. That was what he'd always looked for when he auditioned anyone, that 'special something'. You couldn't define it. It often didn't matter that the girl didn't have a very good voice – if she had that special something she'd be all right. It was like making people laugh. All those great stand-up comics like Frankie Howerd, Max Miller, Tommy Cooper – well, he had a few props – if you read their material it wasn't that funny. It was the way they put it across. How did they do it? He'd often thought about it, but it was a mystery. You couldn't teach it to anyone. It was either there or it wasn't.

But now it had started to rain. He'd have to turn back. He'd been dreading the evening, having to be cheerful among a crowd of people he didn't know. He'd hardly gone out during the five years Ethel had been ill. He'd even sold the car eventually and for the past two years he'd had the groceries delivered.

A waitress held a tray of glasses of sparkling wine for everyone as they came downstairs. He took one, then a loud, rather posh voice said, 'Aha, I remember you! You were here about five or six Christmases ago, weren't you? On your own now I suppose, like me? My husband passed away last February, quite suddenly. We'd been coming here for Christmas for fifteen years, so I thought, why not carry on? Jim would have wanted me to, I'm sure!'

Ah yes, he remembered her now. A very bossy lady with a large bust and an extravagant hairdo; hen-pecked-looking husband. He and Ethel had tried to keep away from her. He smiled at her weakly. He could hardly turn his back!

'Look, all us singles are on the same table together. I'll show you. I can't remember your name, by the way. Mine's Mildred. Milly if you like. I prefer Mildred.'

'Maurice,' he said. But she didn't seem to be listening as she grabbed his hand and led him through a crowd of people into the dining room.

He didn't really enjoy the dinner although there was nothing wrong with the food. Roast pheasant was the main course. Mildred, who sat herself beside him, complained in a loud voice that it hadn't been hung long enough.

'My Jim used to shoot. "Let them hang for a week," he always said. Now this tastes as if it's been hung for only two or three days at the most.'

It tasted fine to him.

'Many people don't like it too high and gamey, you know,' he ventured.

'Well, they should! That's the whole point of having game.'

Oh dear, was she going to be argumentative? He looked sideways at her as she was addressing someone else across the table. She seemed to know everyone. She didn't seem to have altered at all, nor did she seem very upset by her husband's death. The other people round the table were all what is politely called of 'the third age' and he was probably the oldest. In fact, all the people in the hotel seemed middle-aged or elderly, apart from a small party of six people in their twenties or thirties. *Why on earth had they come to a place like this?* he wondered.

And after dinner, the dancing. Mildred was immediately swept off by a military-looking gentleman and Maurice breathed a sigh of relief. He excused himself to the other seven people at the table and made for the conservatory and smoked a quiet cigarette. Some people were going to church at midnight but he didn't think he'd go. He'd only been once since Ethel's funeral. He wasn't religious, but the hymns made him feel sad and he could feel the tears trickling down his cheeks. It was too embarrassing! No, he'd go upstairs to bed quite soon, but first watch the dancing for a little. He'd always loved to watch people dance.

'Aha! Found you at last. Come on, you must give me a waltz or a quickstep before I go off and be holy in church!' Mildred of course!

Oh well! He took the floor.

'Goodness, you dance very well Maurice, almost professional.'

'Thank you,' he said.

'What did you used to do before you retired? You are retired, of course?'

'Yes. First of all I was on the stage and then I was a theatrical manager and agent.'

'Goodness, that explains why you're such a good dancer.'

He couldn't quite follow this but let it pass.

'What did you do on the stage? Acting?'

'No, no. I was a comedian. I told jokes, but I wasn't very funny.'

'I'm sure you were!'

As he took his dinner jacket off in the bedroom he noticed it smelled strongly of Mildred's perfume. She wasn't a bad-looking woman he supposed, but she was very bossy and did talk such a lot.

He thought if he got down to breakfast early he wouldn't have to talk much. Breakfast was a buffet, his programme said, from eight to ten. And sure enough, there was only one other 'single' at the table, a morose-looking bachelor chap of about 65 or so who merely looked up from gouging out his grapefruit from its skin to say, 'Er . . . Happy Christmas!'

Another walk, longer this time, was indicated before lunch, which was to be a cold affair, with a full Christmas roast turkey dinner in the evening. It was a nice fine morning and he must have walked for almost three hours and then went to his room and managed not to sit next to Mildred at lunch by arriving at the very last moment. But Mildred was in full swing by the time he sat down.

'You won't believe this everybody, but do you know, the manager has just told me that we've been let down by the entertainers this evening. No, this afternoon with the conjurer and the puppets is still on, but the Olde Tyme Variety Show they'd booked for this evening have rung to say they're not coming.'

'Oh shame – why?' somebody said.

'I don't know.'

'Always the highlight of Christmas here for me, the variety show in the evening!'

'Yes, me too! Do you think we should ask for a refund?'

'Not the hotel's fault.'

'What shall we all do?'

'Play bridge or watch TV.'

'I do that most nights anyhow. I was looking forward to something different.'

'Look everyone, I have an idea,' announced Mildred loudly. 'We'll get up a show ourselves. I did it once before in the church hall one New Year. It was very good. I expect we've got a lot of talent lurking here.'

'You'll never manage it, Milly.'

'Bet I will. I'll go and ask the manager if I can try.'

'No!' said Maurice as Mildred, with clipboard and pencil, bore down on him a little later.

'Now don't be like that, Maurice. I've already got five volunteers and you told me you used to be a comedian.'

'Yes, but a very bad one. Anyhow, it was years and years ago.'

'Well come along, I'm sure everyone will laugh. It will be Christmas evening after all.'

She put her arm around his shoulders and snuggled her face near his cheek.

'Be a dear. Just for Mildred.'

Once again that perfume!

'Oh, all right. About three or four jokes if you want. The trouble used to be, you see, that nobody ever laughed much. That's why I became an agent.'

Oh God, why had he agreed to do it? He sat in his bedroom dressed again in his dinner suit and looked out at the sea and the stars. It was a lovely clear Christmas night and he wished he was back in his flat in Ealing on his own. It would be even better if Ethel were there! He'd rehearsed a few jokes in his mind. They were awfully old and everyone must have heard them before. And maybe he'd finish with a song. He still had quite a good tenor voice but it would have to be something without any high notes!

Ethel would have said he was a fool.

He tried not to drink too much during dinner. But perhaps it would have been better if he had. He was feeling awfully nervous. Mildred had produced a programme which she'd photocopied and doled out to everyone as they seated themselves in the main lounge. The platform, which had been successively used by the dance band, the conjurer and the puppeteers, was now lit by two spotlights.

'Shhh!' said Mildred in a loud voice and, switching out the main lights in the lounge, she mounted the platform in what was undoubtedly meant to be a skittish manner. She had on a long, bright red evening dress with sequins round the collar and cuffs.

'As you all know,' she announced, 'we have been let down by our Olde Tyme Music Hall artists, so we must entertain ourselves. We have ten sporting volunteers, as on your programmes, so please give them a big round of applause in advance . . . And you never know, we may discover a star in the making . . . So here goes with act number one, Geoffrey "The Pelvis" Elvis.'

Geoffrey was a middle-aged man. He carried a cassette recorder which he placed with exaggerated care on the platform. He then pressed a button and quickly removed his spectacles and slicked his hair across his forehead as the sounds of 'The King' burst forth from the cassette at full volume. He proceeded to mime to 'Let Me Be Your Teddy Bear' followed by 'Heartbreak Hotel'.

Maurice thought, *Well, he isn't very, very bad, just, well, quite bad.* He wondered why on earth Geoffrey had brought the cassette player and the Elvis tape with him for his Christmas holiday. Perhaps he always did his Elvis imitation for his wife on Boxing Night in the privacy of their bedroom?

Maurice noted that he himself was number nine on the programme, before the final number, which was 'Mildred will play a few old loved favourites at the piano and we hope you will join in!'

Turns two to eight varied from the embarrassing to the pathetic. A lady sang – very badly – two numbers from Gilbert and Sullivan, but Mildred's accompaniment at the piano was really quite good, thought Maurice. A younger man tried to do some imitations of various TV and political personalities and finished with what was supposed to be the Prime Minister. Not very convincing.

Maurice's heart gradually sank lower and lower. For some reason he had never felt so nervous in his life. But why? Everyone clapped at the end of each act, even when it was really dreadful. It was Christmas night after all – the season of goodwill. His mind must have wandered because he suddenly realised that Mildred was standing on the platform and saying, 'Come along Maurice. Where are you? Don't be shy. Do I have to come and drag you up here? Ha, ha, ha!' She thereupon did a dramatic leap from the platform and shimmied her way towards Maurice, who was sitting at the rear of room, and grabbed him by his hand. There was a great deal of tittering and applause as she and Maurice mounted the platform.

'Now go on, tell us some jokes, Maurice, as you said you would. And I hope they're not too rude!'

He realised now what it must have felt like for those young people he had so often auditioned. Moist under the armpits, dry in the mouth and throat, and the heart pounding. He should have been much nicer to them. He saw himself standing there in the spotlights, a thin man nearing eighty in an old baggy dinner suit with an old-fashioned straight-back haircut, his hair nearly white, spectacles and a toothbrush moustache. And he knew that his voice would have that odd Cockney twang in it when he started speaking, as it always did when he was nervous.

'Well,' he began, 'this one is about the vicar's parrot. No, sorry, that's wrong. The vicar didn't have a parrot, the lady he was coming to visit had just been given a parrot. No, sorry, two parrots. Both the same.'

A large lady in the front row started laughing very loudly. It was more like a cackle. 'Yes, she'd just been given two, a male and a female, same breed and she didn't know which was which you see. So she asked her neighbour, Mrs Smith, how to find out.' Pause . . . some tittering. 'Well, the neighbour said, lowering her voice, "It's simple. You wait for the one to get on the top of the other and then you'll know he's the male." So she waited and of course it happened just as she saw the vicar coming up the front garden path to visit her. Well she didn't know what to do. She didn't want the vicar to see the parrots . . . well, like that . . . so she quickly opened the cage, knocked the male off the top of the female and tied her white lace handkerchief round his neck to identify him. She then shut the cage and opened the front door and in walked the vicar in his dog collar. At which the male parrot uttered his first words, "Hello, so you've been caught at it too, have you?"'

Oh dear! There was a silence . . . nobody had understood. It was too crude. And then slowly the lady in the front row burst forth with the most raucous laugh. She put her head back and hooted. And slowly everyone else started laughing. He remembered, 'Give them 30 seconds . . . no, a little longer' . . . then, 'That reminds me, talking of clerical things, a man decided to become a monk, a Trappist. They're only allowed to speak once a year. Well, the first year came round and the

Abbot asked the monk to speak. "I'm thirsty," said the monk. The next year came round and the Abbot asked him to speak again. "I'm hungry," said the monk. The third year came round, "I'm leaving," said the monk. "Thank goodness for that," said the Abbot, "you've done nothing but complain ever since you've been here."'

The cackling lady laughed so much she seemed to be in a state of collapse. What had he said? Only an old joke. Oh well, give them at least 30 seconds . . . everyone was laughing.

'Artist to picture dealer, "I painted this picture to keep the wolf from the door." Dealer, after surveying it critically, "Well, why don't you put it by the door so the wolf can see it."'

The lady actually slid off her chair and lay on the floor at this. Maurice thought she'd obviously had too much to drink, but everyone else was laughing too. And so it went on.

Five minutes later he'd given them all the jokes he'd thought of in his bedroom and he realised for the first time in his life that he had held his audience completely. But how on earth was he going to finish off?

'I will finish with a seasonal one. A vicar again. No, no parrots this time – only the Sunday School. It was Christmas and the vicar showed the children a picture of the nativity. The inn, the stable, and in the sky one large bright star. "Look at the star," said the vicar. "What does it tell you?" A little boy put up his hand and said, "It means it isn't a very good inn. Otherwise it would have three stars."' He didn't wait for the laughter . . . 'But we are lucky, aren't we? We're here in a three-star hotel at Christmas, and not only is it Christmas, it's the seaside. Come on, Mildred, you must know this one, help me along, everyone join in. "Oh, we do like to be beside the seaside . . ."'

He finished feeling supremely confident. He bowed graciously to Mildred to thank her and then to the audience three times to acknowledge the applause, and left the platform at something approaching a run. As he passed through the lounge the applause was amazing. Even some of the waiters were standing at the back, no doubt attracted by the laughter. One patted him on the shoulder as he passed and said, 'Jolly good, sir!'

He went out into the conservatory to light a cigarette and cool off. He could just hear Mildred at the piano and everyone singing. What a funny business! He sat down on a cane chair underneath one of the palm trees and took out his handkerchief and wiped his brow. 'Ah well, Ethel. Not such a fool maybe!' he said, addressing the palm tree. But why? Why had they laughed so much? It was almost sinister. Mass hysteria, like when Princess Diana died.

One of the young men had also come into the conservatory for a smoke. He saw Maurice and rushed forward with his hand outstretched.

'Wonderful stuff, sir. Jolly well done. Haven't laughed so much in years.'

All Maurice could say was, 'Thank you.'

He thought it would be best to go up to his room. He wasn't very good at accepting praise. He'd never had much during his life. He lay down on the bed. Well, he'd managed somehow to make them laugh. He got up and pulled back the curtains and looked out across the sea. It was very calm and the sky was full of stars. He thought of his flat and would have liked to have gone home at that moment. But tomorrow was Boxing Day and he wasn't due to go home until the day after. There wouldn't be any trains on Boxing Day anyhow. Oh well! There was a knock at the door. He supposed he'd better open it. It was Mildred.

'Ah Maurice, I just wanted to say you were wonderful. Thank you, thank you.' She put her arms round him and buried her head on his shoulder. That perfume again!

'It's kind of you to say so, Mildred. It all went very well, didn't it, thanks to your organisation,' he said, pushing her gently away.

'Are you just going to stay in your room?'

'Yes, I think so. I'm feeling rather tired just now. I hope you enjoy the rest of your evening.'

He shut the door on her and slowly undressed, then put on his pyjamas and lay down looking at the stars. It seemed he had suddenly acquired that 'special something'. But how he had come by it was a mystery. It had come about fifty years too late. Just think, in his young days he could have had a line of Mildreds queuing outside his dressing-room door!!

He laughed to himself and turned out the light.

Passing the Buck

'It is difficult for me to write this. I was always rather fond of my uncle John, even though he could be stubborn and cantankerous at times. I suppose that was only to be expected from a bachelor schoolmaster. He didn't retire from teaching at our local boarding school until he was 70. He said the headmaster begged him to stay on each year, but my wife and I suspected that John didn't like the idea of moving to a place on his own. He'd always had a flat in the school.

'However, when he eventually retired, he bought himself a very nice little cottage with beams and inglenook and a large neglected garden on the edge of the village in which the school was situated and announced that in addition to reading all his books he'd never had time to read he was going to spend his retirement creating "a wonderful garden – the sort of garden people would pay to visit".

'He showed me a plan of what he intended to do before he started. There was a large area of lawn with a rose garden, a herbaceous border and a vegetable plot. By way of adornment there was to be a pergola and a fish pond with aquatic plants. It seemed very ambitious for someone who had done little gardening before.

'"I intend to do all the work myself," he said, "apart from the initial clearing of the ground. It will keep me fit and busy!"

'Well, three years later, although not fully mature, the garden looked wonderful. He'd taken advice from a local nurseryman about what to plant where, but he'd found all the plants and done all the work himself. The large fish pond must have been a considerable undertaking for a man of over 70 to excavate and line, but I noticed that it was in a slightly different position from the one shown on his garden plan. When I mentioned this to him, he was very brusque.

'"Ah, well, I changed my mind about that. Looks better where it is, I think!"

'After another season, I expected John to start opening the garden to the public. But now he seemed reluctant to do this. First he said he didn't think the garden was quite ready, and then after another couple of years the excuse changed to that he didn't want hordes of children rushing round his flower beds.

'When he was 78 he fell and hurt his leg, which made keeping the garden in its normal immaculate state a great effort. And he refused to have any help. I suggested to him that it was time to call it a day as far as the garden was concerned and possibly he should consider moving into a residential home. There was a very good one nearby and he could afford the fees without having immediately to sell the cottage. But he was adamant.

'"I want to die at Willow Cottage. No homes for me. Lot of old women jabbering all day long!"

'Then early one morning he fell down the stairs. Fortunately, his daily help turned up five minutes later and found him and called the doctor, who lived only two houses away. The doctor pronounced that my uncle had broken a leg and probably cracked two ribs and summoned an ambulance. The doctor told me later that he was astonished that my uncle had made such a fuss about not wanting to be taken out of his house, and as he was carried through the front door on a stretcher, he had tried to grab and hold on to the door post.

'The bones mended reasonably quickly, but the fall seemed to have affected the old man's mind. He became, in popular parlance, a "nutcase". All he kept saying was that he wanted to go home and when anyone tried to reason with him he shouted: "You don't understand!"

'My wife and I consulted the doctor, who was of the opinion that Uncle John would need nursing care for the rest of his life. When I asked the doctor, as I felt I had to, how long my uncle was likely to live, he said it might be for ages. There was now nothing wrong with him physically.

'Whereas the residential home was something that could be afforded out of my uncle's pension and income from savings without disposing of the cottage, full-time nursing care in a proper nursing home would be very much more expensive. The cottage would have to be sold or let as soon as possible, otherwise I could see I should have to make up the considerable shortfall out of my own pocket. I had my uncle's Power of Attorney so I consulted three local estate agents, all of whom were of the opinion that in the current state of the market an unfurnished letting would be the best option. I therefore instructed one of them to let the cottage, or better still, sell it. Meanwhile, my wife Jan and I supposed we'd better go through all the old boy's papers and personal effects before calling in a house clearer to deal with the furniture and fittings, most of which were rather old and dilapidated. We'd done this sort of thing for my wife's relatives twice before and didn't look forward to it. However, we donned old clothes and set out for the cottage on a fine autumn day.

'"You'd better do the downstairs study and living room, Nigel, and I'll make a start in the kitchen. I suggest we dump anything burnable outside the back door and in due course you can light a bonfire," instructed my practical wife.

'So I made a start on Uncle's desk. The top two side drawers were full of old letters in neat piles bound round with rubber bands and I put them in a cardboard box I'd brought with me to look through later. In the middle drawer there was writing paper, pens, paper clips and ink and, somewhat to my surprise, an envelope on which was written: "Strictly Private and Confidential for my nephew Nigel. Only to be opened after my death." Well, I was in a dilemma. My uncle was not dead but he was completely gaga and unlikely to recover. I reflected for several minutes on what I should do for the best. I concluded that the letter probably consisted of some instructions to supplement his will, which I knew was deposited with his solicitors, and was most likely about various small belongings in the house, so I decided I'd better open it. I scanned the two pages written in my uncle's precise copperplate handwriting and whistled under my breath. I went out into the garden and slowly walked past the pergola and the fish pond, both beginning to look somewhat neglected, and sat down on a stone seat. I then read the letter again, carefully this time.

'*My dear Nigel, you were, as usual, bright enough to notice immediately that I had moved the position of the fish pond from where it was shown on the garden plan. The reason for this was, when I started to dig in the original position, I unearthed a skeleton! A foot showed first, and then the rest of the leg. After a day's careful work the whole thing was laid bare. I judged it was of a female as it was only about 5ft 3in tall and the most notable thing about it was that the left hand side of the skull had been bashed in. I suppose as soon as I unearthed the foot and leg I should have immediately notified the police. But I was worried. I thought of what had happened recently when skeletons had been found in other houses! The police would descend upon my cottage, dig up the whole garden and tear the house apart looking for more corpses – no doubt the work of a multiple killer. It would disrupt all my plans for the garden and a quiet life, and would probably make the cottage unsaleable when it comes to be sold. I covered the skeleton with an old tarpaulin and wrestled with my conscience, but couldn't decide what to do. I think I was in quite a state because I impetuously got in my car and drove to see Bill Burgess, my old colleague from school who'd also retired, to talk the thing over with him and see if he could help me. But when I got to his house it was shut up and a neighbour said that he'd gone away on a holiday somewhere and didn't know when he'd be back. I couldn't think of anyone else I could trust with my secret and so reluctantly I drove home and decided I'd have to phone the police. But when I picked up the receiver the phone was dead. It had been working the previous day, but was now obviously 'out of order'. I took Bill being out and the phone being out of order as some sort of omen and I went straight away out into the garden and started to cover the skeleton with earth and fill in the hole. The poor soul had been dead, at a guess, for say 20 years; a few more without a proper burial would not make any difference. There might of course have been other skeletons around the place but the same would apply to them. I hope all this doesn't sound too callous or selfish! So, Nigel, I leave you to do whatever is necessary after I'm dead. I know this seems like passing the buck. And no doubt I shall be vilified a bit in the local press when it all comes to light but I shall have had uninterrupted possession of my cottage and garden. Your affectionate uncle, John.*

'I read the last bit of the letter again very carefully. *Do whatever is necessary*. I knew my uncle always chose his words with care as a classical scholar. I'd assumed that he would leave the cottage to me, but I hadn't seen his will and I didn't think I had the right to ask to see it. The words *when it comes to be sold* were neutral. Perhaps he'd left everything to the school? He knew I was reasonably comfortably off. The real problem was, of course, that my uncle only expected me to read the letter after he was dead and I would then know what was in his will. Oh dear, what a dilemma!

'I shoved the letter in my trouser pocket and went back up towards the cottage. Jan was piling stuff outside the back door.

'"I do wish you'd light the bonfire, Nigel. What are you doing wandering about the garden? We'll never get finished today at this rate!"

'So I found some matches in the kitchen and carried a pile of old newspapers and cardboard boxes onto a bit of rough grass at the side of the house and set fire to them. I then went back to the study and went through the rest of my uncle's desk in case there might be some further communication for me. But I found nothing. I made a decision. I went out and, poking up the bonfire with a stick so that it blazed up, took the letter from my pocket, tore it into small pieces and carefully put each piece on the fire. At that moment, of course, Jan came out of the back door.

'"What are you burning?"

'"Oh, just some of Uncle John's old letters."

'"Good, I'm glad you're getting on. I'll soon be ready to move upstairs to the bedrooms."

'In spite of being slightly interrupted by three sets of people being shown round the cottage by the estate agents, we managed to finish what we'd come to do by the end of the afternoon. I put the cardboard boxes containing all my uncle's letters and other papers in the boot of the car to be looked through later and we drove home.

'When we arrived home, I felt I needed a whisky and was just pouring it when the phone rang. It was the estate agents to say that they'd had an offer from some people to buy the cottage! I immediately told Jan.

'"Oh excellent," she said. "I know you were worried about having to pay the balance of Uncle John's nursing home fees, particularly as you were hoping to be able to retire soon."

'She came over to me and patted me on the shoulder as she always did when she was pleased. Then she sniffed.

'"Goodness, I didn't notice it in the car, but you smell dreadfully of bonfires! I think you'd better change your clothes and have a shower."

'I've written this down in detail exactly as it happened, a sort of confession, to get it off my chest. If anyone thinks I acted to make my life an easy one, it has been anything other than that since then.

'First of all, when I came to draw my pension I found it was much less than I expected. Something had gone wrong with the pension fund. Second, my wife and I were involved in a car crash. My wife was killed. I lost the sight in one eye and injured my right arm so badly that I can no longer play golf. Because of all that, I think, I developed shingles and now I have been diagnosed with Parkinson's disease. I am feeling very, very depressed. Uncle John is, amazingly, still alive but his mind has gone completely. He doesn't recognise me at all any more. My uncle's Willow Cottage burnt down two years ago and four modern houses have been built on the site. I hoped that when they were being built the excavations for the foundations would unearth the body, but apparently they didn't.

'I hope whoever reads this will not think too badly of me.'

A police sergeant was standing in Nigel's bedroom reading the handwritten confession. Nigel's dead body lay on the bed beside it.

The doctor had examined the body and the bottle of pills on the bedside table and announced, subject to a post-mortem, that the deceased had apparently committed suicide.

'I think you're right,' said the sergeant. 'Read this stuff that was lying beside him. It's a long confession, a suicide note I suppose, but the oddest one I've ever read. I shall have to pass it to the coroner. I pity those poor devils who bought the new houses in Willow Close. No doubt we shall be instructed to do what will be called "a thorough search", but it could turn into a demolition job!'

The Stoic

It was a minor media sensation! The popular papers loved it. 'Tessa head over heels', 'The Prof's love nest', proclaimed the headlines.

The more serious papers also loved it in a more restrained way. One of their 'diaries' had this small paragraph:

I understand that Professor Tom Pithy (62), who had such a resounding success with his series The Social Life of Primates *on TV, recently has left his wife of 35 years, the well-known novelist Barbara Pithy (58), to live with the delectable Tessa Avon (24), star of the notable TV costume drama series* The Life of Nelson *and more recently the record-breaking British film* To Sea Afar. *The couple are apparently at a secret hideaway somewhere in Italy.*

And the papers' columnists quickly grasped something new to pontificate upon. The most feminist of them was in something of a dilemma as she wasn't quite sure whether to praise Tessa for her free spirit or commiserate with the deserted wife. So she wrote a rather boring article on father-figure fixation instead.

A liberal male columnist wrote a long and learned article citing various examples from mythology and history of similar liaisons, indicating that there was nothing unusual about them or particularly wrong.

And there was an email sent by a professor in Scotland to a professor in the USA which is relevant to the story.

Dear Bill,

Following your phone call to enquire 'what the hell's gotten into old Tom', I have, as promised, been making enquiries. It appears that about four years ago Tom must have offended someone at the old place where we all toiled together and he was 'eased out' early but given the title of Emeritus Professor of course. He had to give up his rooms in college and go and live with Barbara in that freezing cold old rectory the whole time. You will remember Barbara as a right pain in the neck – or even lower! However, every cloud has its silver lining and out of the blue Tom was asked to do this TV series of which you may have heard but probably not seen. It was very good. Tom's pomposity was just right!

Maybe the experience liberated Tom or maybe he couldn't stand Barbara any longer but he suddenly took up with this Tessa Avon. You have no doubt seen photographs of her if you've not seen her films. She looks a flighty bit of goods to me and what she sees in Tom is a mystery. Tom was never one for molesting young students, unlike some of our old colleagues. Maybe she likes his inflexibility, which you will remember no doubt. Once Tom made up his mind about anything there was no budging him, even if he was manifestly wrong. And he was always banging on about Stoicism. Maybe that's why the college got rid of him. He could be ridiculous at times; but anyhow, one must wish him luck. He's not a bad chap really.

Best, Andrew

Meanwhile, several journalists from the more popular papers, never more aroused than when a hideaway is 'secret', had run Tessa and the Professor to earth, discovering them to be staying in a small villa up a via in Ravello. As ringing the doorbell produced no reply, they camped outside day and night in the narrow via hoping to get a photo of the loving couple or possibly even an interview. After two days, when there had been no sign of either of them, there was speculation among the now disgruntled newspapermen as to whether the couple were living on 'love' or 'fresh air' or 'had a big freezer', until on the third day the grocer's van drew up at the end of the via and the grocer, accompanied by three large Italians in black shirts and trousers and wearing dark glasses, passed several crates of stores, food and bottles through the front door, the three large Italians forming a guard round the doorway to keep the journalists at bay.

After another week only three very determined journalists, including a photographer, lingered and their patience was at last rewarded when a taxi drew up at the end of the via blowing its horn violently and a few minutes later the Professor and Tessa rushed out of the front door and into the back seat. The photographer managed a shot of the couple looking extremely displeased. By making enquiries of the other taxi drivers at the taxi rank and distributing euros to them, the journalists found out that the Professor had hired the taxi to go down to Amalfi, so it was not long before they were snooping around the front at Amalfi. And their persistence was rewarded when they spotted the Professor sitting on the beach helping Tessa undress for a swim.

'Oh, for God's sake, piss off and give us a break!' the Professor remarked in an unacademic manner as the journalists approached. In the meantime, Tessa rushed into the sea and disappeared under the water. The photographer, smacking his lips at the prospect of a shot of Tessa emerging in her bikini dripping from the waves, began to patrol the water's edge, while the other journalists pestered the Professor with questions such as 'Does having a young girlfriend make you feel tired?', which he refused to answer. He lay silently on his back in the sand exposing his grey hairy chest to the sun. He then closed his eyes and feigned sleep, adopting the stoical pose for which he was noted.

The Professor and Tessa had met because they were placed side by side at a celebrity charity dinner in London one night. The Professor looked very handsome in a rather old-fashioned dinner suit and Tessa delectable in a dress which was almost transparent. The Professor had always been rather shy with young women in flimsy dresses, but found himself completely at ease with Tessa, who told him how much she'd liked his TV series and questioned him closely about the research for it. The Professor was at some disadvantage as he hadn't seen Tessa on the TV and was only vaguely aware that she was some sort of film star.

'I haven't come with anyone and I get very nervous in the dark. Could you possibly see me home, Tom?' Tessa asked at the end of the evening.

The Professor replied, 'Of course.' He was not going home to Suffolk; he'd booked a room at his club.

He was rather surprised, however, to be invited into Tessa's flat, which was large and very untidy in an obscure part of South Kensington, for a cup of coffee. The rest was inevitable. The Professor vaguely wondered as they grappled in bed whether she was a nymphomaniac, but decided he really didn't care. He found her irresistible. When he woke up in the morning, she had become an obsession.

*

Tessa appeared delighted at his suggestion that they should go away together and live somewhere abroad. They both had ample funds from their recent successes. The Professor chose Ravello because he'd been there before, thought that the weather would be good and that it would be a very suitable place to hide out. And Tessa agreed because the name Ravello sounded romantic! They were very happy at first. They ate alternately at two very nice restaurants and no one appeared to recognise Tessa, who had scraped her long blonde hair back into a bun and always wore large sunglasses. And then the English journalists arrived!

After the first trip to the beach, and for a few days afterwards, it was rather fun making bolts for a taxi with the reporters giving chase. But soon the photographer had enough photos to sell and the reporters were obviously not going to get any further information, and they all disappeared. The Professor had to admit quietly to himself that he missed not being the centre of attention. He started vaguely sorting through some of his papers which he'd brought with him. They were notes for a new book. Tessa lay under a sunshade on the terrace, sleeping a good deal and painting her finger- and toenails while gazing down at the sea and the wonderful view.

And then one day a large packet arrived.

'What is it?' the Professor snapped.

'Oh, nothing!' said Tessa. But he grabbed it from her and as he looked at the envelope and where it came from, a strange numbness came over him. 'It's a film script, isn't it? I thought we agreed no work!'

'But you've started to look at your notes!'

'But that's different!'

'No it isn't.'

She took the script and went and sat down on the terrace and started to read it.

The Professor was devastated! He had somehow thought that the idyll would go on for ever. But of course she'd want to 'do' something sooner or later. And if he prevented her there was a strong chance that he would lose her. A thought which filled him with dread.

And so, over dinner, the conversation went like this.

'Well, was it a good script?'

'Yes! Absolutely right for me. My agent must have organised it and told the producers where I was.'

'So you really want to do this picture?'

'Yes, I think I am too young to give up working, Tom.'

'Where is the filming to be?'

'Hollywood and a small bit on location.'

'How long will it take?'

'I suppose only three to four months. It's a short script. But you can never tell exactly.'

'Well, you must go and do it!'

'I didn't expect you to say that.'

'Why not? We're told these days that the wishes of the individual are paramount and you must do what you want.'

'Oh don't be upset, Tom. I want you to come with me and be by my side during the shooting.'

'Much though I should like to be with you, my dear, I can't think of anything I should like less than hanging around a film studio day after day doing nothing. I had some experience of it when I was doing my TV series.'

'But you wouldn't be doing nothing. Couldn't you be writing your book?'

'Of course not. I need total peace and quiet with my notes and I couldn't possibly concentrate with the background noise of the studio.'

'But they could put you up in a soundproof room or something.'

'Don't be silly. You know they couldn't and wouldn't. No, if you must go and get on with your work, I must get on with mine here.'

He thought Tessa looked very sad.

And so the arrangements were made. They hired a car to take her to the airport at Rome. On the way he said, 'It's going to be difficult us being apart, but it will be a test. Other people have done it successfully and maintained a relationship and in fact it is often stronger after a time apart. I suggest rather than trying to phone or even Skype each other all the time we only speak once a week. I think that would be better. Do you agree?'

'If that's what you want, Tom.'

She was not normally very emotional but he noticed she was crying as she said goodbye before going through passport control and check-in.

And he felt very sick in the car on the way back to Ravello, but once there he wrote down a plan for his days in the future. Up at seven and a few exercises or maybe a walk or a jog. Breakfast. Work until lunchtime – snack lunch in the villa. A short nap until four, and then more work until it was time for a drink and to go out to dinner. They'd never had a TV but he bought himself a radio so that he could listen to the World

Service in English, and he did have the diversion occasionally of buying a London paper when he took half a day off and went down to Amalfi.

For several weeks he and Tessa spoke on their mobile phones on a Sunday when she wasn't filming. She seemed to him to be a little distant but quite happy, and she assured him that the filming was on schedule and said she was looking forward to coming back.

And then one Sunday when he phoned he couldn't get any reply.

'Ah, gone on location. No signal!' he thought.

The very next day he went down to Amalfi, where the only English paper he could find was the *Daily Mail* for the previous Saturday. There, on page 2, the *Mail* proclaimed: 'Tessa's new love', and there was a picture of her hand in hand with the male star of the film she was making.

The Professor's first reaction was one of disbelief; sure that it was a publicity stunt by the studio. But all the way back to Ravello on the bus he became less sure. Every day he tried several times to reach her on her mobile phone, but without any luck. He thought of contacting the studio; but no, he couldn't stoop to that!

Trying to block the whole thing from his mind, he bought a small laptop and started typing his book.

The tourist season was almost over and it was getting chilly at night. He was halfway through the book. He'd fallen into the habit of having a grappa after dinner in the restaurant. One night while he was drinking it, he saw a copy of *Hello!* magazine which a party of Americans had left behind at the next table.

He picked it up and idly skimmed through the pages full of laughing and self-satisfied celebrities. And then he turned a page and stopped. 'Tessa Avon pregnant,' proclaimed the headline. And there was a photo of Tessa standing sideways to the camera with her hand on her stomach and with her co-star grinning at her side with his hand over hers!

He closed the magazine and took several deep breaths. If she was publicly saying she was pregnant then the pregnancy must have happened very soon after she'd arrived in Los Angeles! He knew the baby could not be his. Early in their marriage, after a miscarriage which had made her extremely ill, Barbara had insisted that he had a vasectomy.

He staggered home in a daze, sat down at his desk and tried to carry on typing where he'd left off. But he kept hitting the wrong keys. He went and lay down and tried to sleep, but he couldn't. After the emotions of rage and jealousy came the self-blame. He was not used to admitting that he had made mistakes, but he saw now that if he had gone to Hollywood with Tessa this would never have happened. He remembered how she had cried at the airport. She must have thought he was trying to get rid of her, and it had been compounded by his only wanting to speak on the phone once a week. What a fool he'd been! This was a judgement on him. He did not sleep at all that night.

Early the next morning he walked round the town trying to decide what to do. The smell of coffee and hot pastries from the cafés made him feel for the moment that life might still be worth living and he sat and had his breakfast outside one of them. Then he started to weep – something he had never done before in his adult life. But he was not sure if he was crying at the loss of Tessa or at his own pig-headedness. What could the future hold for him now? He didn't want to go back to the mud and cold of his home in Suffolk even if Barbara was prepared to have him! Anyhow, she hardly ever spoke to him. She just sat at her word processor obsessionally writing her latest novel!

His own book? Well, it was all right but somehow he had no enthusiasm to finish it. Another TV series? Well, nobody had asked him to do one.

There was no way back. The stoics knew how to deal with situations like this. The example of Cato the Younger came to mind. He had no sword but there were other ways.

So, later on, he visited the local doctor and, complaining of insomnia, obtained a prescription. That evening, he went out to dinner at his usual restaurant and afterwards had not one but three grappas. Returning home, he took Tessa's photograph from his desk and threw it into the dustbin. He then swallowed all twenty-four sleeping tablets and calmly lay down on his bed, having first drawn back the curtains so he could look at the moon, which was almost full. At first the moon shone brightly, but then a cloud began to obscure it and presently a gentle rain began to fall. But the Professor was unaware of it and would not be troubled by earthly things again.

The Recompense

'Hi, Julian – over here!'

I looked up from pushing my trolley in Marks & Spencer's food department and saw a tall lady gesticulating at me. She was a little hampered in doing this as she had a plastic cup of coffee in one hand and a mobile phone clamped to her ear with the other.

At first I thought I would take no notice. Julian is my name but I did not think I knew the lady or liked the look of her. But on second thoughts, which I later regretted, she did seem vaguely familiar, so I duly pushed my barrow towards her. As I approached she yelled into the phone, 'Hang on a minute, dear, I've just met an old friend,' and put it on top of her shopping so that she could embrace me with the arm that wasn't holding the coffee.

'You don't recognise me, do you? It's Marcia. You did my divorce for me years ago.'

It came back to me. Yes, I thought it had been a rather successful outcome for a very difficult client. I couldn't remember her surname though.

'I thought I might bump into you,' she continued. 'I looked you up in the phone book and saw you lived round here. I've been in the States for years. Just over for a short holiday – borrowed a flat from a friend. Well, I'd better finish my phone call and let you get your shopping done. Catch you later!'

As I continued pushing my trolley round the shelves I remembered more about Marcia. Although I had thought the divorce settlement was very advantageous for her, she had not seemed particularly pleased.

'Ah well, I'm sure you did your best, Julian,' she said several times.

And she had been a stamp collector. Strange for a woman, I thought, although I know the Queen is one. Somehow it had arisen in conversation that I too was a philatelist and had a quite valuable collection. After that, every time we met she quizzed me about what stamps I had. I found it rather intrusive.

I didn't hurry my shopping. It was horribly hot outside on the King's Road and I found the chiller cabinets wonderfully cooling. I thought she'd forgotten about me as I didn't see her again around the shelves, but there she was waiting for me with her bag of shopping by her side at the end of the checkouts.

'Ah, Julian, there you are at last! It's wonderful to see you again after all these years and a happy chance for me as I'm having trouble with the bank I'm using over here. Do you think you could just have a quick look at the letter I've had from it and tell me what to do? I don't have anyone here to advise me.'

'Well, I'll do my best,' I said, 'but you must understand that I retired from practice some while ago.'

'Of course; but just as a favour for an old friend. Look, why don't you come round to my place for a drink either tonight or tomorrow?'

I didn't really want to go but I supposed it could do no harm. I am a bachelor and my life has been a little lonely since I retired.

'I could come this evening I suppose, before dinner, maybe about six o'clock.'

'Lovely! Look, I've written my address on this slip of paper. I'm sure you know where it is.'

The address showed that the flat was in Dixon Court in Chesham Street, Belgravia, not a very long walk from my place in Cadogan Gardens, but it seemed far enough in the oppressive heat. I reflected that it had been very foolish of me to return to London from the country so early in September. I normally leave it until the 1st of October.

Dixon Court turned out to be a dreary-looking block built after the Second World War, no doubt as the result of bomb damage.

'Come up, second floor,' her voice rang tinnily out of the entryphone. 'I'm afraid there isn't a lift.'

She met me at the door wearing a strange Indian-style flimsy dress and a great deal of perfume.

'Shall I get you a gin and tonic with lots of ice? God, it's hot isn't it, just like New York. Make yourself comfortable on the sofa over there and for God's sake take off your jacket, and your tie as well if you want. You lawyers are so formal!'

While she disappeared into the kitchen to get the drink I glanced round the flat. It was hot and stuffy, sparsely furnished, and had the air of not having been lived in for some time.

I had just taken two sips of my gin and tonic and was about to ask the usual sort of polite questions such as 'How long are you staying in London?' when the entryphone buzzer went. This seemed to fluster her.

'Oh God, I hope this isn't . . .' she said to me, and then into the entryphone, 'John! . . . Of course, come on up,' and then to me, 'For God's sake, quick, get into the spare bedroom behind you and lock the door. It's my new lover – hideously jealous! If he finds you here no amount of explaining will convince him. Whatever you do don't come out until the coast is clear. He could be violent.'

Ten seconds later I was locked in a cupboard-like bedroom. It was at most five feet by six feet in size and had nothing in it but a single bed and a wardrobe. It was even stuffier than the rest of the flat. I didn't like to try and open the window as it might make a noise. I put my head to the door and could hear Marcia talking with a man, although I couldn't make out what they were saying. They seemed to be arguing at first and then there was a bit of laughter and then I heard glasses clinking and the conversation became sporadic. As there was nothing else to do, I lay down on the bed, tried to convince myself that I didn't feel claustrophobic, and waited.

I woke with a start and looked at my watch – it was 8.15 and getting dark! What was or wasn't happening next door? I wondered. There was no light showing under the door and I couldn't hear any movement. I felt I couldn't wait for ever. Maybe they'd gone out or perhaps were in bed together! I turned the key quietly and opened the door of the bedroom and tiptoed into the living room. When I had first come in there were Marcia's belongings all over the room. A handbag, shoes, shopping. Now the place was completely tidy. The only sign of humanity was my jacket on the back of the chair where I had left it. I peered into the bedroom. It was equally tidy. There were no dirty glasses in the kitchen!

How strange! I began to have forebodings. I went to my jacket and felt for my wallet. It had gone! It had had a considerable amount of money in it and all my credit cards – not that they would be of much use in these days of chip and pin! Then I felt in the side pocket of my jacket. My keys were missing!

I let myself out of the flat without difficulty. They had not locked me in! I ran down the four flights of stairs, out of the front door and into the street. Arriving back at Cadogan Gardens some ten minutes later dripping with sweat from the heat and anxiety, I roused the caretaker, who gave me my spare set of keys so that I could let myself in. As I thought, I had been very neatly burgled, and of course my stamp collection had been taken.

There was a little note propped on my desk.

This makes up for what you failed to get for me before! M.

Escaping

Maggie still couldn't stop crying, although Doug had been buried three weeks. She kept seeing him lying face down in the farmyard, his body surrounded by the white pellets from the sack he'd been emptying into the fertilizer spreader. They said he'd had a heart attack. But he must have lifted hundreds of those sacks before! It wasn't fair. First she'd lost the baby – and now Doug. She didn't believe in God any more. And the Colonel, who owned the farm, was asking her to take this new worker as a lodger in her farm cottage.

She didn't want a lodger, but she'd been wondering how she'd manage without Doug's wages and didn't want to upset the Colonel. She might lose her job cleaning for the Colonel's wife! The last thing she wanted was to have to go home to her mum in Glasgow and share a room with her sister, who wasn't quite right in the head.

So she agreed.

But she was a little frightened of the new man. He was tall and dark and growing a beard. He seemed very glum when Maggie showed him round her cottage, which was only a few yards from the seashore. There was a dismal kitchen with a solid-fuel Aga, a sitting room with a tortoiseshell fire, and upstairs two bedrooms. The bathroom was in a lean-to off the kitchen. The bedroom at the rear of the cottage, which was to be his, looked towards the grey North Sea and was decorated with bright yellow wallpaper covered with teddy bears and balloons. The only furniture was a baby's cot.

'I lost the baby, ye see,' said Maggie. 'The Colonel's promised to get me some furniture and we'll see about the wallpaper. Seventy pounds a week, a cooked breakfast, a packed lunch, and a cooked tea.'

The man was already regretting his drunken and furious departure from his home, shouting, 'You can have everything. You'll never see me again!'

Once he'd left home he realised that he'd left his passport behind and had only £200 in cash in his pocket and was not going to be able to use his chequebook or credit cards if he didn't want to be traced. But he was determined never to go back.

He'd come on the night sleeper to Scotland because his mother had been Scottish, and looked for work on farms because she had been a farmer's daughter and he'd often helped on the family farm in Perthshire when he was young, and had loved it.

But the Colonel's farm was so bleak. Down a narrow lane, it was five miles from the nearest town, just grazing land rising slowly from the east coast; cattle and sheep and lots of sea mists. The lane had only five houses in it and it petered out into a rough track and then a footpath along the shore. But unlike other places he'd tried, the Colonel had made no difficulties about his lack of identity, or the fact that he didn't have a P45 and wanted to be paid in cash, after he'd explained that he was getting away from domestic troubles. He'd convinced the Colonel that he knew about farming and could also look after the Colonel's garden.

He and Maggie said little to one another for the first few weeks. He had difficulty in understanding her thick Glasgow accent. After his tea he went out for a walk along the shore, but as autumn set in and it was too dark to walk, he wanted to read in his bedroom. His bedroom had no heating so he asked Maggie if he could please read his book in the kitchen by the Aga in the evening. He knew she always went into the sitting room to watch the TV.

'Ay, course ye can, if ye help with the washing up.'

Maggie became intrigued by the man, who said his name was Fraser, but she didn't believe it was his real name. He always called her Mrs Mullins – very polite! He had a slight Scottish accent. But she thought he was putting that on! His beard had grey in it, so she thought he must be over forty.

The man tried never to think of his elegant dining room in London and cellar of fine wines as he ate her meals. She was not a bad-looking little girl and seemed kind-hearted. He put her in her early twenties. She was sturdily built with stocky legs and an ample body. Her face was small and pale and surrounded by a mop of black curly hair which was often in need of a wash. He kept telling himself he was glad he had made the break, but earning enough money by this way of life to try and buy himself a new identity was depressing. His body ached from the unaccustomed manual work. He would have sunk into even deeper depression had he not seen Fiona.

'Who is that girl I see walking her dog down the lane every day?' he asked Maggie one evening.

'Ay, that's Fiona Walker. Lives in the next house on the right up the lane. She's come back from nursing in Edinburgh to look after her mother who's ill. D'ye think she's pretty?'

'No, no. I just wondered who she was.'

'She's very toffee-nosed. She wouldn't look at a farm worker, I can tell ye.'

But he more than wondered who Fiona was! He watched out for her in the lane and when he was in his room during the day on Saturdays or Sundays. He noticed she often took her dog, a West Highland White, onto the beach and played ball with it. So, trying to appear nonchalant, he took extensive weekend walks by himself along the beach in the hope of meeting her. The more often he caught glimpses of her, the more attractive she seemed. She was the total opposite of Maggie. Slim, tall and refined-looking, she had bobbed red hair and walked very primly.

Two Sundays later, after his lunch, he was taking his usual stroll along the beach. It was very cold and still. He walked disconsolately along the water's edge for some time, letting the waves trickle up to his boots and back. He was looking out to sea at two men in a boat in the far distance and wondering what they were fishing for when suddenly he heard, 'Will! Will!' He turned and there was a dog tearing across the beach towards him with Fiona in pursuit. But she didn't know his name! Nobody knew here that he was called Will!

The dog arrived and splashed into the sea and jumped at his legs. Only then did he realise that the dog must be called Will.

Fiona arrived a few seconds later, panting and looking rather pink in the face.

'Sorry, he's not very obedient I'm afraid. I hope you're not too wet.'

All he could think of saying was, 'I thought someone was calling me.'

Fiona looked into his face in a puzzled way.

'My name's Will, you see, or at least some people used to call me that.'

'Oh, you're Fraser, aren't you, from the farm? Come over and sit here on the rocks. I need a rest! You lodge with Maggie Mullins, don't you? And you're a bit of a mystery, aren't you?'

'Am I?'

'Nobody knows who you are or where you came from, and you certainly don't look or speak like a farm hand.'

'No, maybe not.'

'So you're not going to give me a clue?'

'No, I don't think I can.'

'All right, be unfriendly then!'

'It's not that. I certainly wouldn't wish to be unfriendly, particularly to you, but I really can't say any more at the moment. Maybe I can tell you one day.'

She looked at him very keenly for such a long time that he began to feel embarrassed. He feared that maybe she'd recognised him from photographs in newspapers, in spite of his newly grown beard. But she said nothing and suddenly got up, calling the dog, who was snuffling around in some wet seaweed nearby.

'Can't you stay and talk a little longer?' he asked.

'No, I'm afraid I must get back. Mother's ill and on her own.'

She did smile briefly as she turned and left.

Then a few days later, when he arrived home from work, there was an envelope for him on the kitchen table addressed to 'William Fraser'.

'Yon Fiona left it for ye,' said Maggie, coldly nodding her head towards it.

He tore open the envelope.

'I'm sorry if I was rude to you. I'm worried about Mother, you see. Our kitchen garden needs tidying and digging. Could you possibly please come and do it for us? You can turn up more or less any time – provided it's not dark! Fiona Walker.'

But Maggie, he noticed, was glaring at him.

'Y'er looking very pleased with yerself!'

'Yes, it's an offer of some work in the garden.'

'Oh aye. Well ye'd better get cleaned up – yer tea's nearly ready, or, no doubt, as they say in England, where they tell me you've been living, yer dinner.'

'I couldn't help living in England.'

'If ye say so.'

He went to do Mrs Walker's vegetable garden at the first opportunity, which was the next Sunday morning after he'd finished his feeding duties at the farm. He asked Maggie for some sandwiches instead of his usual cooked Sunday dinner, which she seemed none too pleased about. He went to the back door of Mrs Walker's house just to say he was there. Fiona answered it. She was dressed in a beautiful green tweed suit and had dangling pearl earrings.

'Ah, Will. As you'll see I'm away out to a Sunday lunch. Mother's got her helper with her. I'm sure you'll know what to do. All the tools are in the shed over there. I'll probably be back before you're finished. Tidy up what's still there. Pick some sprouts for tomorrow's lunch and dig over the bits that are clear. Okay?'

He smiled and bowed his head.

By three fifteen, Fiona was back.

'I left early,' she said, as she came to look at what he'd done.

'God it was awful. Presumably you don't remember about Scottish Sunday lunches as you've been living so long in England, I hear.'

'Word travels fast.'

'It's a very enclosed community round here. Everyone knows what everyone else is doing. So you must remember that and watch what you say, although I gather you don't ever say much anyhow.'

'No.'

'When you've finished, come inside and we'll drink some tea and have a chat.'

Later, his arrival in the kitchen was greeted by furious barking by Will the dog.

'Now be quiet, Will. This Will is a friend, remember?' said Fiona.

So he sat in the kitchen feeling rather uncomfortable in his working overalls while Fiona made the tea and poured it into beautiful china cups. She looked very elegant, he thought, in her tweed suit as she walked around the kitchen. She sat down opposite him and looked at him levelly.

'Are you still not going to tell me who you really are?'

'I'm sorry, no. How's your mother?'

'She's not at all well. I think Christmas and the New Year are going to be very difficult, otherwise I'd ask you for a meal as Maggie's going to be away.' She looked at his startled face. 'Ah, she hasn't told you yet?'

'No.'

'I'm sorry. Look, I'm going to have to leave you for a moment to see Mother and relieve the helper. Take another cup from the pot if you want.'

'You're very kind, Miss Walker, but I must go now.'

'If you must. I haven't any cash in the house to pay you. I'll let you have it later.'

As he walked slowly back down the road two things struck him. The first was that Fiona was almost schizophrenic in her manner: one minute friendly, the next minute dismissive. Very odd. And second, it really was true, everyone knew what everyone else was doing in the lane. And he was going to be on his own for Christmas!

He walked back into the farmyard very sadly. Fiona obviously didn't like him that much. She was just intrigued about who he was. Morosely, he leant over the bars of the cattle shed and the bullocks, who were lying down, gazed mournfully back.

So he spent Christmas and the New Year in the cottage on his own. Maggie had gone to Glasgow to see her mother and sister, but first she hired a taxi to the supermarket in the town to buy enough food for him while she was away, as well as presents for her family.

'Ye'll be able to cope on yer own, I ken,' she said.

He wasn't so sure. It was a long time since he'd cooked a meal for himself. However, Maggie had stocked up with everything she said he would need. He offered to pay for the Christmas pudding and the mince pies and the chicken and the ham which Maggie insisted on getting him as a 'Christmas treat'. She also wanted to buy him some beer or wine and whisky. But he refused. He'd given up drinking completely to save money and didn't want to start again.

And everyone else went away. The Colonel and his wife to Barbados until the New Year, and the other farm workers to their families, leaving only himself and Fred, the farm foreman, and his wife. And Fred announced that he would only work on the 27th and 28th of December. This left him to do all the feeding on the other days, including looking after the chickens and the dogs and the cats. In spite of all the activity, he had to admit he felt very lonely and at a loose end.

Maggie came home on the evening of the 3rd of January. It was very cold and has started to snow. A taxi brought her from the station. He had just come in from work and was lighting the fire in the sitting room for Maggie's arrival.

Maggie was almost unrecognisable. She'd had her hair done into tight curls and brought herself a completely new set of clothes: a bright red short skirt, along with a black jumper, black tights and red high-heeled shoes.

'I've been to the sales! How do I look?'

'Er, very nice!'

He was taken aback and slightly aroused by the sight of Maggie all dressed up like this.

'Have ye had yer tea?'

'No, not yet.'

'Good. I stopped off and got us some fish and chips. And look what else I've bought.' She reached into her bag and brought out a litre bottle of whisky. 'It's for the New Year. Come on, ye must have a drink for the New Year! I'll put the fish in the Aga to keep warm while we have a dram. I hope ye've kept it alight okay.'

Maggie sat herself down at the kitchen table, grinning broadly, and half filled two tumblers with the whisky. He'd not tasted any alcohol for months, and after the second of what Maggie called 'a good Glasgow dram' he felt completely drunk, in spite of eating the fish and chips and having the inevitable cups of strong tea. He wished he hadn't agreed to drink. But he'd been very, very lonely over the holiday period.

'I'll clear away but we'll no do the washing up till later,' Maggie said. 'Go and sit down and turn on the TV.'

And now he was sitting on the sofa vaguely looking at a Christmassy programme and nodding off to sleep when suddenly he realised Maggie was sitting close beside him and holding his hand.

'Have ye no missed me? I've missed you! Is it no cosy just you and me?'

She put her head on his shoulder. He froze. While he'd nodded off he'd been dreaming about Fiona!

'Do ye no like me? Look at these!' She rose and pulled her new black jumper over her head, revealing her naked bosom.

'Good God!' he thought. She must have taken her bra off in the kitchen.

'Yon Fiona will no be able to give ye anything like these!'

Maggie bounced them up and down a bit, then fell on top of him on the sofa. He had no idea that this was going to happen. He twisted round and stood up.

'And don't say ye don't like them!' she cackled. 'That's no a pistol I can see in yer trouser pocket.'

'Good God, I need a bit of comfort,' he thought.

He went and sat down beside Maggie and lay his head on her chest.

'That's better!' she said, putting her arms around him.

He felt so inebriated he didn't really care what they were

doing, either on the floor by the fire or later in Maggie's bed. But when he woke up at about five thirty the next morning it all seemed somewhat different.

'I've a wee hangover. Have ye no one too?' asked Maggie.

He agreed that he didn't feel too great, but wondered to himself whether it was in fact a hangover or feelings of guilt.

And Maggie said at breakfast, 'Instead of calling me Mrs Mullins, ye'd better go on calling me "Maggie" or "darling" like ye did last night.'

And as he went out of the door she shouted after him: 'And no more seeing Fiona!'

It was very cold outside and snow had settled to about two inches deep. But as he walked across the road, who did he see immediately driving into the farmyard before anyone else had arrived but Fiona! She skidded to a halt in her small Fiat, jumped out and ran up to him.

'Ah good, I hoped I'd find someone around. Please come with me. Mother's fallen over outside and I simply can't lift her up the steps to the back door. I've called the doctor, but he's out seeing someone and the Colonel didn't answer when I phoned. Mother will freeze to death if she's not got inside.'

Of course he immediately got into the Fiat beside Fiona, who drove off rather wildly with the car skidding all over the road.

Mrs Walker was lying, as Fiona had said, where she'd tripped and fallen at the bottom of the steps to her back door, face down in the snow. Fiona had put a blanket round her mother and a cushion under her face.

'She must have been trying to feed the birds or something absolutely daft. As you can see, she's only got her nightdress on! I've examined her and I'm sure she's not broken anything.'

Slowly they got Mrs Walker into the kitchen and made her comfortable in a chair, where she sat groaning while Fiona told her mother how silly she'd been.

'I ought to get back, I think. I should have started work by now,' he said.

'Oh, please stay with me until the doctor comes. I'll get some more blankets and some hot water bottles for Mother and make some tea. And then I'll phone the Colonel or his wife and tell them what's happened.'

So he sat and had tea with Fiona and waited for the doctor to come. It was ten o'clock before he arrived back at the farm for work.

'Difficult to know what to do today, Fraser, with all this snow. But I've got a few jobs lined up for you. However, I gather you've already done a good job on Mrs Walker!' said the Colonel.

So he spent the day carrying out various tedious little jobs the Colonel had given to him, thinking all the time how wonderful it had been to see Fiona again and what on earth was he going to do about Maggie?

When he arrived home for his tea, she was waiting for him in the kitchen and it looked suspiciously as though she'd been at the whisky bottle again. Her little face was red and she glowered at him and picked up the bread knife and waved it about.

'I told ye no to speak to Fiona again, didn't I? And what do ye do straight away? Get off with her in her car!'

'But it was an emergency. Her mother had fallen over in the garden in all the snow and she wanted help lifting her indoors.'

'Well ye could have got someone else to go with her. I told ye no to speak to her again.'

'Don't be so silly, Maggie!' he shouted as Maggie came towards him brandishing the bread knife. He grabbed her hand and easily twisted the knife out of her grip, from where it dropped onto the floor. Deprived of the knife, Maggie still came on and tried to scratch his face. And when he grabbed both her hands she just lay against him sobbing.

'I canna bear it if ye speak to her ever again. Promise ye never will!'

She was hysterical. He tried to calm her down by stroking her hair. The evening was spent with Maggie saying, 'Why don't ye promise?' and him saying, 'It's unreasonable and impossible,' until eventually he got her into her bed and sat beside her on it holding her hand. Part of him would have liked to have got in beside her as it was so cold, but he knew he mustn't. So he sat and shivered.

'Are you going to be able to sleep, Maggie, do you think?'

'No. There's some sleeping tablets in the cupboard in the bathroom that I got from the doctor after Doug died. Ye'll see them there. Bring them and I'll take two.'

Eventually, having taken the sleeping pills, Maggie went off to sleep. When he was sure she was unlikely to wake, he tiptoed out of the room and into his own bedroom. But he didn't get into bed. He quietly gathered his things together and, packing everything into his small backpack, let himself out of the front door.

It had been snowing again during the evening, but the snow had now stopped and the stars were shining. It all looked very pretty indeed. But he was running away again, and he'd no idea where to. He'd never given his wife another thought since the day he'd walked out, but he did now think about Maggie lying asleep and hoped when she woke up and found him gone she wouldn't take the rest of the sleeping pills which were still in the bottle on her bedside table. He should have taken it away!

The Wrath of God

The man who sold him the dinghy said:

'You're new around here, aren't you, sir? Be careful of the tide when you take her out. It's not too bad up river, but from here downstream the current's very strong when the tide's running.'

'Ah, yes, I'll be careful. Don't worry,' replied Alec.

The boat seller watched him hobble away with the dinghy oars over his shoulder and the rowlocks in his jacket pocket and hoped he would be all right. Tall, very thin, with sandy hair turning grey, he didn't look very robust or well.

Alec had now taken the dinghy out several times up river. Apart from the difficulty of getting in and out of the boat because of his bad legs he'd managed pretty well. He'd been born and brought up in Scotland and he was used to rowing boats on the lochs. Up river was quite pretty, but now he'd like to try down the estuary to the mouth. He chose a day when the tide was high at three o'clock and he reckoned he should manage the whole round trip in just under an hour. The June sun shone brightly overhead, but it was not too hot rowing as there was a breeze off the sea. At first, the tide was still coming in and he had to pull hard just using his arms as his legs had no strength in them. Soon the water was almost still and his oars left pleasing expanding rings astern. He supposed he should now feel more content, as having the boat encouraged him to get out of the house. But he didn't.

Once again, he started thinking about what had happened over the past year. Morag kept telling him, 'Don't dwell on the past. Look to the future. Our luck will change!' But it wasn't easy. He'd always imagined his retirement to a villa in the south of France with a smart yacht in a marina nearby. But here he was, retired at 58, rowing a small second-hand dinghy down a muddy east-coast estuary in England and living in a two-bedroom cottage. None of the things that had gone wrong were his fault. For years after moving south he'd worked hard and made a good living as an insurance broker in and around London. People thought they were dealing with an honest man with his pleasant face and Scottish accent. But then more and more people started to use the Internet for comparative quotes. Then came the credit crunch and his business had suddenly dwindled. So he decided to retire early. As he'd always paid the maximum contribution into his self employed pension fund he thought he'd be reasonably well off, but he'd patriotically invested it all in shares in the Scottish banks and everyone knew what had happened to them. They'd lost about 90% of their value quite suddenly, almost overnight. What a disaster!

'Never mind!' Morag had said when she knew how small their pension would be. 'This house in Weybridge should be worth quite a bit. We'll sell it and move to something small in the country, and invest the balance. We can live on that.'

But of course property prices also fell and the best rate of interest he was able to get for the surplus money was three per cent. No wonder he'd been ill. He thought at one stage he was going to die. Now his legs wouldn't work properly. He couldn't walk far and thus wasn't able to play golf, which is why he'd resorted to buying the boat. He felt so low that most of the time he really wasn't interested in anything. His GP had put him on antidepressants.

We are much affected by our early life and he'd often wondered if God was punishing him, although he could hardly believe it. He'd had a very puritanical upbringing. The minister at the kirk had always taught that God smiled on those who helped themselves and worked hard. That was probably why he'd been so successful in insurance. But he couldn't get away from the fact that just before his business had started to fall away he had committed adultery. Adrienne was so attractive that at the time he felt he couldn't have helped himself. But the minister would have undoubtedly have said that Adrienne was a 'painted Jezebel', and his warning that 'the wrath of God shall fall upon fornicators' kept coming back to Alec. And of course adultery was worse than fornication – it was a breach of one of the Commandments.

His musings were interrupted by a shout from behind him.

'Ahoy there!'

He turned round and rested on his oars. The shout came from a large seagoing yacht which was anchored near the bank. Just the sort of boat he'd imagined himself owning in the south of France! There was a man in the stern dressed in smart white trousers and an open-necked blue shirt, with a red cravat tucked in at the neck.

'Ahoy!' the man shouted again. 'Are you local by any chance?'

'Well, yes,' Alec shouted back.

'We've just put in here for the night and would like to go

ashore this evening for some drinks and something to eat. Could you advise us on the best place to go?'

'Well, the pub I go to, the Anchor, is quite good. But people say the food at the George Hotel is better.'

'Look, old chap, why don't you paddle over and come aboard for a few minutes so we can chat about it rather than shouting at one another?'

'Fine!' Alec shouted back.

He was rather pleased to find someone who wanted to chat. He was finding it difficult to make friends in the little town, and it would be nice to have a closer look at the yacht.

Two minutes later he'd managed to tie up his dinghy to the yacht.

'Welcome aboard,' said the man, giving Alec a helping hand. 'I'm Desmond Hanniford. Let's have a drink while we talk, eh?'

'Well, a cold drink would be very welcome, thank you. Lovely boat!'

'Yes, not bad is she? But wait till you see my current crew. They're sunbathing on the top deck . . . Come down, girls. Make yourself decent and look lively, we've a visitor who needs a drink. He's been rowing.'

Alec felt his jaw dropping with amazement as two absolutely stunning girls came down the steps onto the aft deck. They'd obviously been sunbathing nude and were fastening the tops of their bikinis.

'The girls don't speak much English. The blonde one on the left is my First Mate and the dark one on the right is my Second Mate. Quick, girls, grog for the gentleman!'

Desmond, on closer inspection, appeared very bronzed and fit, with a wide smile and a mouthful of very white teeth.

Definitely Errol Flynn on his yacht, Alec thought. He felt himself very scruffy, dressed in his old jeans and tatty shirt with a threadbare collar. He'd stopped bothering about what he looked like since he'd been ill.

Alec explained that he was a newish resident, but did his best to give Desmond a description of the three pubs and the grandish hotel, though he could hardly keep his eyes off the two girls, who returned with a tray with glasses and a tall jug full of a greenish-coloured drink, with a large number of ice cubes floating in it. The First Mate gave Alec a glass to hold, and as she leant over, Alec had a wonderful view of a suntanned cleavage. The Second Mate followed behind to pour the drink from the jug, and as she did so she put her hand over his hand that was holding the glass, as though to steady it, and she smiled the most beautiful smile.

'The girls are coming ashore as well. That's why they're putting on their war paint!' Desmond said a bit later, nodding his head to where the girls were now sitting on the side of the yacht, painting their finger- and toenails.

Alec wondered how on earth Desmond, who was probably about seventy, had got these girls. They must be some specialised sort of prostitutes, advertised as 'crew girls' or something similar, he surmised.

But Desmond was saying something.

'So, Alec, you say you go to the Anchor every night at about six for half a pint? Why don't we meet you there? We could make up a nice foursome. How about it?'

The sudden thought of an evening with the Second Mate entered Alec's mind. He looked across at her, and particularly her thighs, as she sat carefully painting her toenails a bright scarlet. The colour went very well with her dark blue bikini, her tanned skin and her brown hair. She must have felt him looking at her because she looked up and smiled at him again.

'Splendid idea!' replied Alec. But suddenly he noticed that the yacht was turning at anchor and facing upstream. 'But look, I must be paddling back. I see the tide's turning,' he said with a nonchalance born of the alcohol he had just consumed.

He attempted to get up from the folding chair he was sitting in, but found it strangely difficult. That grog must have been practically neat gin!

The Second Mate quickly came over and helped him up. She held his arm and took him to where his dinghy was tethered, then squeezed his hand as she helped him down into it, saying, 'I look forward to ze evening.'

He felt elated and inebriated as he rowed away strongly. He wondered what lie he was going to tell Morag that would enable him to spend the whole evening away. The alcohol and his elation helped him make good progress, and soon he could see the landing stage over his shoulder about 250 yards away. But suddenly he realised that the dinghy was no longer moving! He checked his position against the post on the bank and then rowed with all his strength while he silently counted to two hundred. Then he looked up. He was in exactly the same place! He was never going to make it back to the landing stage. *Give it another supreme effort*, he said to himself, and rowed until his head was aching and his heart pounding. But it was no good. He suddenly felt in a state of collapse and knew he was going to be swept out to sea by the tide. The dinghy would undoubtedly capsize when it got to the sea and he would be drowned as he couldn't swim properly because of his bad legs. He stopped rowing and got up to turn himself so that he would be facing the bow and the direction in which the dinghy was now travelling. But his legs gave way and he went sprawling into the bottom of the boat, hitting his head on the thwart. As he fell, he heard the minister's voice coming across the water:

'Ye have heard that it was said by them of old time Thou shalt not commit adultery. But I say unto you That whosoever looketh on a woman to lust after her hath committed adultery with her already in his heart.'

When he opened his eyes his first thought was 'the wages of sin is death', but he must still be alive as he could smell the paint, heated by the sun, on the thwart. Painfully he turned his head to left and right. There, to the right, was the estuary in the distance. He must be nearly 500 yards out to sea.

What had happened was a further warning! He hoped he would be rescued soon as the sea was calm and Morag would tell the coastguard that he was missing. He must be patient and wait. There was no point in trying to start rowing to the shore; he felt too ill. He shifted his body so that he lay in the bottom of the boat on his back looking up at the sky.

He thought, 'I must try to be better in future.' But try as he might, he could not stop having visions of the second mate's thighs as he looked into the beautiful blue sky above him.

Salvation

Today was his 50th birthday and it was very hot, as it usually was on 24th June in London.

As he walked down the six fights of stairs from his flat, he could feel his shirt beginning to stick to his back under his lightweight jacket and regretted putting on a cravat. Outside, although it was only nine o'clock, the heat rose from the pavement as he made his way round the corner to the café where he always had his breakfast. For once, he didn't start to read *The Times* that he'd bought from the shop next door immediately on sitting down. Today was a day to think about things, to take stock.

Well, it wasn't really his birthday at all. His actual birthday was tomorrow but he'd adopted the 24th of June as his 'official' birthday. It seemed a better and more memorable day. The 24th of June – Midsummer Day. It had a romantic feel to it. He'd first been taken with the idea during his very brief and abortive legal studies. Some old leases, he had learned, had a rent of 'a rose at Midsummer', which was a variation on that oddity a rent of 'a peppercorn'. He couldn't imagine anyone actually giving his landlord a peppercorn, but a rose at Midsummer to a gracious and smiling landlady was a pleasing notion. A red rose, undoubtedly.

The quarter days were very odd. There was 25th March,

Lady Day – the jolly old Annunciation – and 29th September, Michaelmas, and of course Christmas Day. But why weren't they all on the *25th*? And the summer quarter day was on 24th June – the birthday of John the Baptist. He remembered once on his official birthday going into Siena Cathedral to light a candle – because it was his birthday, and there was this notice in Italian and English, saying, 'This way to the relic of St John the Baptist.' So he went and looked at it. It was a skeleton of an arm in a glass case. 'Bloody hell!' he'd exclaimed under his breath and made quickly for the exit. It was ghoulish and incredible and made him feel slightly sick. Once outside in the cathedral square, though, he'd remembered what his very religious father had always said to him when as a teenager he'd got so cross about what he called 'the nonsense of religion'.

'You shouldn't take everything too literally! It's faith and the ideas that matter.'

But all this was getting him nowhere, he realised, as his orange juice, coffee and croissants arrived. Take stock! Literally, that's what he'd resolved to do. The stock market had crashed and showed no signs of recovery. His shares were now worth roughly half what they had been. Interest rates had fallen too. Sixty per cent of his money was on deposit at a variable rate of interest and was now only earning about 4.25%. Goodness, at one time it had been 7.5%! So his finances were not in good shape. He'd hardly enough income to live on without resorting to capital and he'd have to do something about it!

He hadn't worked for the past twenty-five years. He should be grateful for that. After Cambridge and the very short abortive law course, he'd taught in an awful boys' prep school for two and a half years. All right if you liked little boys. He didn't! The worst bit had been when the head had approached him and asked him to teach French.

'Well, Headmaster, my French is very basic.'

'Never mind, Horatio, at least you can keep order. All those bloody Froggie French masters I get are hopeless. I can hear the row from the French room here in my study. I'll pay you extra, of course.'

And because he'd been hard up, he'd agreed. It was terrible! He did keep order, but in every form there seemed to be an awful little beast who obviously had a French mother or granny or something who ran rings round him! What a relief when his father had died and he'd inherited – well, so much that he'd been able to give up school-mastering. He'd sold the big old family house in Hampshire and bought himself a flat in South Kensington. He'd invested the rest of the money (not too wisely, it seemed now!) apart from ten grand, which he'd set aside to buy some nice pictures. He'd always wanted a picture collection. Once he'd resigned his job, he'd done nothing for several months and it proved so blissful he'd decided it should be his future – the life of a leisured gentleman, watching cricket, going to races, the theatre, concerts, parties. If you didn't have to work, why do it?

And then there were the pictures.

He'd started to go to Christie's auctions just down the road and he had the time to go to the innumerable art galleries in London. He'd read about art and painting extensively. Overall, he had an idea that he would be able to buy a picture or two very cheaply by someone famous. Something that everyone had overlooked because it was unsigned. However, the more often he went to Christie's or the dealers in St James's, the less likely this seemed. So he started going to small country auctions where pictures were only a part of the mixed bag of furniture and bric-a-brac. Then suddenly, when viewing a row of very uninspiring pictures one day in a small town in Sussex, he gasped. Surely it was a Picasso, or was it somebody trying to be like Picasso? He looked at the uninformative catalogue. 'Lot 203 – Head of Man' was the only description. It was a small sketch with, of course, one eye below the other. Surely, he thought, Picasso always signed his pictures? Well, maybe Picasso forgot this one. He stood at the back of the auction room.

'Lot 203 – Head of Man. Will somebody start me at fifty pounds?'

He put up his hand. There was no other bid. Obviously that was just above the reserve price. Well, if it was a Picasso, he was in luck. If it wasn't, he'd only lost fifty pounds. When he got it back to the flat he'd undone the back and taken it out of the frame and there, under the mount, was the signature! He was told it was genuine and, now reframed with the signature showing, it was hanging in his living room together with his two other scoops, both picked up for practically nothing as well. He loved them all. Not only because they were what they were, but because they were worth such a lot and cost such a little! But the insurance premiums were beginning to be a problem.

And then he remembered the less, much less happy occasion when he paid way above the estimate at Christie's for a large oil painting. He could have guaranteed at the time it was by somebody much more famous than the attribution. He couldn't bear even now to name the name! He'd taken it to be authenticated and he'd been told that he was surely wrong and Christie's had got it right! He didn't try any more scoops after that. He just made a nice little collection of Victorian watercolours. They sat very well with the three scoops.

But once again he realised that he was not really 'taking stock'. The real problem was money. He could sell a painting or he could try to get a job if anyone would have him at his age – though he really wasn't qualified for anything. He'd hate to teach again. But, ah! . . . Either Vera or Astrid might somehow be the solution. He considered them in turn.

Vera he'd met at a dinner party; sat next to her. Undoubtedly he'd been showing off his knowledge of art somewhat as Vera had said to him as they were leaving that she didn't know anything about art but would love to learn and could he perhaps teach her a bit if they went to the National Gallery together? This was a bit of a come on, he thought, particularly as Vera had mentioned during dinner that she was a widow. The 'winsome widow', he'd come to think of her. Anyhow, he'd arranged to take her one afternoon to the National Gallery, where they'd start with the Primitive Rooms, and after an hour of that, which he'd stipulated was quite enough, they'd come back to tea at his flat. Vera was probably in her mid-forties and rather running to fat, but a very pleasant and grateful companion. She'd looked a little askance, he'd thought, at the dust and untidiness of his sitting room, but was of course greatly impressed by the story of his scoops. During tea she mentioned that her husband had left her well off, but that she wouldn't mind getting married again! Lunch at her house on the Thames near Hampton Court followed shortly. It was quite a nice large, modern house, but furnished in what he considered execrable taste – curtains with swags and flounces, big imitation leather sofas, and glass-top coffee tables everywhere. Each one had a crochet-work mat and a table lamp with an extravagant shade. The lunch was (oh God!) vegetarian with rather sweet tepid hock to drink. After lunch, during a walk along the riverbank, Vera had suggested once again that she wouldn't mind getting married again. She'd helped in her husband's business, which was now sold, and was trying to fill in her time by taking up golf and bridge. Did he play? Inwardly shuddering at the thought of either, he'd replied quietly that he was afraid he did not.

Well, obviously Vera would be willing and it would solve the financial problems, but she'd never want to come and live with him in his flat; he'd have to go and live in that awful house. No. It simply wouldn't be worth it. Vera was a non-starter.

And then there was Astrid – younger and more attractive physically, but perhaps not so good financially. He'd only met her a few weeks ago at a party in Chelsea. It was a warm evening and the guests had spread themselves outdoors into the small garden. He saw Astrid standing under a hanging jasmine holding a half-empty glass of wine and looking forlorn. It was probably the smell of the jasmine that had attracted him to her.

'Hello – you're looking sad!'

'Am I? Well, I don't know anyone apart from the colleague I came with and she's met someone. She's over there.' She nodded, indicating a man and a girl in very close conversation.

'Oh dear. Well, then I'd better talk to you, hadn't I?'

He'd learned that she was a 'keeper' – or was it an 'underkeeper'? – of some era of porcelain – he still could never remember which – at the Victoria & Albert Museum.

'That's a coincidence. My father died years ago and left a small collection of china. He always said it was valuable, but

I've no idea. I think it's Wedgwood. I've always meant to get someone to look at it and tell me what it really is.'

'I'll look at it if you like.'

'Oh, would you! How kind. What shall I do? Shall I bring it into the museum? I'm a bit afraid of breaking it, even though I only live nearby.'

'If you like I'll come and look at it at your house.'

So she'd come and looked at his china and said it was very nice, but only worth a few hundred pounds. She did not seem to mind that the china was very dusty and the flat untidy. He had, of course, been unable to restrain himself in recounting the story of his scoops. Astrid had replied that he was 'wewy, wewy clever'.

'Look, I'd like to thank you for looking at my china for me. Would you let me take you to this concert that's coming up on Friday week at the Cadogan Hall? It's the Mozart Players.'

'Oh wather. Lovely,' she replied. 'Absolutely wipping!'

The fact that Astrid couldn't pronounce her r's was rather endearing at first but became increasingly annoying as time went on. But she obviously liked him a great deal. She came for lunch or supper almost every week now. It seemed that love had passed her by. She was 32 and lived with Mummy in a big house in Dulwich. Daddy had died two or three years ago and she hinted had left her a 'nice little twust fund'. While he sat back confidently in his armchair, she always sat forward on the edge of the sofa looking at him earnestly and appealingly while they discussed art, music and literature very seriously. He'd never touched her. He thought it might lead to all sorts of things that he hadn't then wanted.

'Oh God,' he'd thought after she'd gone the last time, 'I'm just playing with her.'

He was being unfair. Really, he didn't want any involvement.

But what about the money? he asked himself again and again as he walked back home and up the six flights of stairs to his flat. He ripped off his jacket and cravat and rolled up his shirt sleeves and sat down. He'd thought when he woke that morning that he'd go for a walk in Hyde Park and look at the Serpentine and maybe see a nice girl or two bathing. But it was far too hot for walking. He'd just sit there and visualise the walk and think about the money problem while he did it. He'd just about reached the Serpentine in fantasy when he had a thought – 'Oh God' – Astrid was coming to supper that night and he'd have to go out – again – into the heat sometime and collect the Dover sole he'd ordered from the fishmonger. Later! For the time being a little music to help the thought processes! Radio 3 – *The Times* said merely: '10 a.m. – 12 noon Schumann.' He switched on and lit his first Villiger cigar of the day. It was Schumann's piano concerto. Very romantic stuff. As you listened, you always thought you were coming up to the edge of a great mystery or revelation, but then it never quite made it. It was a bit like his feelings on his very occasional visits to nearby Brompton Oratory.

But he wasn't making any progress with what he should do! It was getting very hot in the sitting room. He pushed the sash window fully open. There was a bit of noise from the traffic, but also a very welcome slight breeze. That was better! Make some black coffee . . . it might spur things along . . . While he drank the coffee he looked at the Picasso, the Turner and the J.S. Cotman. Somebody must have died in each case and some distant relative cleared the house and just sent everything to the local auction rooms and the auctioneer had not paid much attention.

He shook his head. *No, I can't bear to part with any of them!* he thought. Really, Astrid seemed the best proposition. He'd have to try and find out a bit more about this trust fund and whether it looked promising, then ask her to marry him. He got quite excited by the idea. She could come and live with him and it would be convenient for her job. They'd have her salary as well as his income plus anything from the trust fund. But then he thought, 'She might want to have a baby. That would be awful! I'd have to put my foot down about that. Anyhow, there's no room for a baby here and there are those six flights of stairs down to the street!' And he hoped two people in the flat wouldn't get in one another's way. But Astrid was quite thin and she'd be out at work all day. So it would probably be all right. She wasn't really bad looking. Her legs were a trifle too thick and her hips a bit broad and her bust, well, disappointing. But her sad face, with its fair hair all around, looked really quite pretty when she smiled. And maybe she wouldn't want a baby anyhow. Better talk to her all about it tonight! It was a particularly romantic bit of Schumann now and he could picture himself sitting beside Astrid on the sofa and maybe holding her hand. But he'd better carefully rehearse the questions about the trust fund, living in his flat and the baby, so that he put them in the right way and in the right order – but she would probably be so eager that she'd agree to anything he wanted. No babies would mean birth control of course. But he supposed he wasn't really a Catholic any longer and anyhow there was a majority of the committee at Vatican II in favour. It was just that the popes didn't like it. He could see their point of view – theoretically.

As it was his birthday he'd lashed out on some caviar for

them to have that evening before the Dover sole. But what he'd do now to celebrate his decision about Astrid was to open a bottle of champagne (they could finish any that was left this evening) and have just a little of the caviar for lunch, followed by an omelette.

Such concentrated thought had made him feel very hungry and the lunch went very well. The caviar was delicious! He'd eaten more of it than he should and there wasn't really enough left for the evening. Never mind, he'd pad it out with some blinis. And he'd drunk the whole of the bottle of champagne! Well, the heat made one thirsty. After he'd listened to *The World at One* on the radio, he'd go out and get the fish, but first a little cognac and one of his best cigars.

He remembered turning off *The World at One* as it was finishing and tapping the ash off his cigar and then he must have dozed off. He was having a dream that he was in hell, or was it purgatory? He could feel the flames round his legs and he expected at any moment the demons to come at him with pitchforks, like in the old religious paintings. His father was standing above him and haranguing him, shouting something about Kant's 'Ultimate Imperative', to 'treat every person as an end also and never as a means only.'

He woke up coughing. Oh God, the place was filled with thick acrid smoke and it was pouring out of the open window. The rug under his feet was on fire. He must have dropped his cigar into the wastepaper basket! He could hardly see across the room. He was going to be burnt alive. He got out of his chair and tried to shout for help. But it was no good, he was choking to death! Savagely, he tried to beat out the flames with a cushion, but only succeeded in burning his hand, scorching his eyebrows and hair, and setting fire to the cushion . . . Then there was the sound of a fire engine outside and a fireman's helmet appeared at the open window.

'Hang on, mate,' the helmet shouted. 'You'll be all right. We'll get you out.'

The fireman was over the sill and had wrapped him in a blanket and hoisted him over his shoulder in no time.

'Just you, is there?'

'Yes, just me,' he coughed.

Horatio lay on the pavement wrapped in the fire blanket and thanked God he'd been rescued. He watched another fireman go up the ladder with a hose and start spraying water into his living room through the window and realised that his flat and all his belongings . . . his pictures … would be ruined.

'You all right, mate?' said the first fireman to him. 'We've called an ambulance.'

'Yes, but my things . . . my flat . . . my paintings . . .'

'Well, I expect it's all insured, isn't it?' said the first fireman cheerfully.

At that stage he must have passed out because the next thing he knew he was lying in bed in a hospital ward. There seemed to be bandages around his head and chin and both his hands. He felt terrible.

Soon, he saw a familiar face. It was Astrid looking solemnly and closely at him. She patted one of his bandaged hands, causing him to wince.

'Oh Howatio,' she said. 'Oh deaw, oh deaw. I came to see you but your flat was in wuins. Thank God you wewe saved!'

'Yes, somehow . . . But I'm confused about it. Is my flat a total write-off?'

'Yes, I'm afwaid so. The west of the building is all wight though.'

'Oh good.'

'It's your biwthday, too. But they say you'll be out of hewe in a few days!'

Horatio mumbled something in reply. What on earth was all this about? Why had it happened? He'd been selfish, but not so as to deserve this. And anyhow, Astrid might have been happy about his asking her to marry him. He'd lost everything apart from his investments . . . And he could see it all – the insurers refusing to pay up because they said it was his fault for dropping his cigar while asleep after heavy drinking!

At this point Astrid put her face very close to Horatio's bandaged one.

'Oh, I do love you, Howatio. It's tewible that this has happened. You'll have nowhere to go. I'll must ask Mummy, of course, but I'm sure it will be all wight. You must come and stay with us as soon as they let you out. We've got tons and tons of woom and I could take time off wowk to look after you.'

Tears of self-pity trickled down his cheeks and into his bandages as Horatio imagined his life at Astrid's mother's house in Dulwich (he'd been there once). Everything neat and tidy. Having to go into the conservatory or the garden to have a smoke. Mummy and Astrid fussing around him. And tea and cornflakes for breakfast!!

Seeking Paradise

I was somewhat late in arriving for New Year's Eve at my sister's. She had recently moved from Ealing in London and she and her husband were now living in a small 'arty' community by the seaside, where my brother-in-law was setting himself up as a potter. After thirty years working for a bank, he had resigned the previous Christmas and announced that he was 'going to pot'. All this, no doubt, had something to do with the fact that our mother had died and left my sister a large amount of money. I had, of course, also benefited, but the last thing I wanted to do was to change my lifestyle. Being a Chancery barrister suited me admirably.

I was very intrigued to see Margot and her family's new way of life and annoyed when my train from London was delayed and I had to wait around in a cold and dark station yard for a taxi. Then the driver had some difficulty in locating Jersey Cottage, which was near the bottom of a very steep lane at the edge of the town.

'Roland, at last!' my sister greeted me, opening the front door and letting out a blast of hot air into the cold night. She was much altered. She had let her greying hair grow and was wearing an odd-looking smock over a pair of black trousers which had sequins sewn down the side of each leg.

'It's all right, we haven't started eating. We want to spin it out until the New Year. But we've had plenty to drink. Come and have some mulled wine.'

I should explain that my sister and I are totally different. Everybody tells me that I'm reserved and fastidious, whereas she is like an enthusiastic Labrador! They were all seated around an enormous fire in the living room. My brother-in-law, Edwin, was clad in a shaggy sweater with corduroy trousers and sandals – a change from the banker's suit or sports coat and flannels at the weekend! The three late-teenage children were looking like, well, all teenage children, in jeans and strange tops. They grinned at me in unison. And then there was a girl with bright red hair and a pink face. The pinkness of the face I deduced was from her sitting too near the roaring fire. I assumed she must be my nephew's girlfriend. But then my sister was waving in her direction and saying, 'This is our neighbour, Rosamund. She's an artist.'

Rosamund smiled at me shyly and lowered her eyes. I glanced at her briefly while she did so. Not bad looking! Rather short and perhaps dumpy, but it was difficult to tell as she was wearing a tent-like green velvet dress.

'Give him a glass, Edwin. No, perhaps you'd like to go upstairs and wash? It's very cold upstairs I'm afraid. We haven't much heating yet – hence the big fire. Your room is on the right.'

As I went upstairs with my case and the cold hit me I thought that although Margot's clothing might be different, she hadn't changed in character – still bossy and trying to get me to do two things at once! How was she managing in this house with no heat? The semi-detached in Ealing had always been far too warm for my taste and almost claustrophobically tidy. Mid-life crisis for both of them, maybe?

Having deposited my case in my room and had a quick wash, as instructed by Margot, I carried downstairs the various Christmas presents I had brought with me in my suitcase – of necessity small and light. But they seemed to be appreciated. Margot appeared to have gone arty with her food too, because the meal consisted of a huge rabbit stew with vegetables, followed by 'some of our local cheeses'. I recalled how on similar occasions in Ealing it would have been smoked salmon followed by roast pheasant. My nephew and two nieces, all of whom were studying at various universities or colleges, kept winking at one another during the meal. When I enquired if they liked the new place, the eldest, Robert, replied that it was great but they wouldn't be here much.

Rosamund said practically nothing.

After supper, Margot organised us in a very silly game called 'Consequences' and then at midnight we all had to sing 'Auld Lang Syne' by the Christmas tree. Then, 'Come on you lot, clearing up and washing up. I don't want to see all these dirty dishes when I come down in the morning! Roland, would you please see Rosamund home. She's afraid of the dark. It's only two hundred yards away up the lane. I'll give you a torch.'

So, clad in our overcoats, Rosamund and I stepped out into the cold blackness of a moonless country night. I shone the torch.

'Which way?' I asked her.

'Down the path and then turn right.'

She clutched my arm. I don't like physical contact and the two hundred yards uphill seemed like a mile. An owl hooted, causing her to gasp and to cling to me even more tightly. And then my torch picked out the eyes of a rabbit in the lane, at which she screamed. It did occur to me that if she was really so afraid of the dark it was a pity she didn't live in a place with street lighting!

Eventually we reached her front door.

'Please come in while I turn on some lights.'

It was a pretty little cottage, very untidy, with an easel, paints and canvases at one end of the large downstairs room. There were other canvases around the walls.

'Would you like to have a look at some of my work?'

As it was nearly one o'clock and well past my usual bedtime I replied, 'That would be lovely, but perhaps tomorrow morning – the light would be better!'

She seemed very disappointed and pouted.

'All right,' she said. 'I'll call round for you.'

And there she was at breakfast the next morning in a smock just like Margot's. I'd spent a wretched night in a freezing cold bedroom trying to get warm and go to sleep and I was not in the best of tempers.

'Have a cup of coffee, Rosie,' said Margot. 'Roland will come round with you as soon as he's finished his breakfast, won't you Roland?'

It made me cross that I was being pushed around again. After breakfast I wanted to clean my teeth and say my prayers, as was my custom. But I'd always found it easier in the long run to give way to my sister. So, after consuming a bowl of porridge and a cup of coffee, I found myself reluctantly walking, more sedately this time and several feet apart, beside Rosamund up the lane. I could hear the sea in the distance and there'd been an early morning frost which was only just disappearing. Everything looked rather nice, I thought.

'A new year and a new start. That's what I always say,' said Rosamund. 'I've tidied up a bit since I knew you were coming.'

And indeed the clutter of last night had all been cleared away.

'Goodness,' I thought, 'she must have been up early!'

'You know I'm not an expert,' I said.

'But your sister said you were very keen and that you went to a lot of exhibitions.'

'Yes, that's true.'

I gazed around the room. The walls were now covered with canvases and there were more propped up by the skirting board. They seemed largely abstract, with a recurrent theme of a house surrounded by green sea. I was not very taken with them, but one has to be polite and make intelligent comments.

'Very nice,' I said, 'but personally . . . for me . . . too abstract. Have you not thought of being a little bit more representational? I don't know what it's called – "abstract expressionism" maybe?'

'I don't know!' She pouted again. She was really rather pretty when she pouted. 'You may be right,' she admitted. 'I've only been out of art school for a year, you see, and I'm still feeling my way.'

'Do you exhibit frequently?' I asked.

'Only at the local gallery. Nothing in London or anything like that.'

'Well, thank you,' I said half an hour later, after I had examined every picture.

I'd found the atmosphere in Rosie's cottage rather intense and I was glad to get back to my sister and her family. My nephew, Robert, was splitting logs and the two girls, Betty and

Jo, were stacking them, all of them, of course, under my sister's watchful supervision.

'Have to keep them at it before the holidays are over. We'd freeze without a big fire alight all the time. Edwin's got plans to put an Aga in the kitchen and run central heating from it, but I don't suppose he'll get round to it, he's so busy with his pottery.'

And Edwin did indeed seem obsessed with his new venture. He hardly ever left his pottery, which was in the garden, except to eat and sleep. I was entertained largely by Margot, who took me for long walks around the harbour and along the beach and cliffs. It was a nice old town, built more or less on the side of a cliff, and the walking was very steep. My knees ached terribly at the end of our walks.

'I'm glad you like our new home and way of life, Roland!' she said as I left (though I hadn't in fact commented on either). 'Come down to see us again at Easter, won't you? The courts don't sit then, do they? And I hope by then Edwin will be ready to show you his work. I'm sorry he's been so secretive about it at the moment.'

And so I went back to my way of life as a barrister, with my flat in the Temple and my chambers across the other side of Fleet Street in Lincoln's Inn.

Easter was late that year and it was thankfully quite pleasantly warm when I re-entered my sister's house. She seemed very pleased to see me. She explained that she'd not made any close friends, apart from Rosie. The children were apparently not coming home for the Easter holidays. They were off on some expedition or other. But Edwin, I gathered, was very happy. His pottery was going very well.

'He's nearly got a contract with a shop in London,' Margot whispered. 'He'll be very happy to show you his stuff now. He was a bit doubtful about it before, you see. And of course Rosie's longing to see you again. She says your suggestions about her paintings have changed her life . . . in fact, I think she's taken a great fancy to you!'

Oh dear! I thought.

And indeed, within an hour of my arrival, Rosamund had called. She seemed to have had a character change. She bounced through the front door shouting, 'Cuckoo!' Her long red hair had been pinned up in two coils, one over each ear, and she was wearing a smart pair of jeans and a jumper.

'Roland, you must please, please come and see what I've been doing. You've changed my life . . . It's wonderful! . . . Come on!!'

As we went out of the front door Margot gave me an exaggerated wink.

I don't know what I was expecting, but the change was remarkable. This, I thought, was really very good stuff. One can't explain really good art or properly describe it, but, as I had suggested, she had moved to a much less abstract style and the effects she had created were, I thought, excellent. I was rather at a loss for words. There were only about a dozen new works and these were on the wall. The old stuff had presumably been cleared away to some upstairs room.

'Well, come on, Roland, what do you think?'

'It's wonderful!' I said. 'Congratulations.'

'There, I knew you would like it! You might even buy one, I suspect, for your little flat where you live all alone, Margot tells me.'

'Yes, I might I think, provided they're not too dear!'

'But first,' she said, 'I want you to look round the gardens of a house near here. They're open today and they're lovely. I've borrowed a friend's car for the afternoon as I knew you came by train.'

'Yes, I don't drive,' I said.

She looked at me oddly. 'Not at all?'

'No. I never learnt.'

The gardens were exceptionally beautiful and it was a good time to look round them because the owners had somehow managed to have the daffodils, the pansies, the aubrietia, the wallflowers and the beds of tulips all in flower at the same time. The house was set up high on a hill a little inland from the sea and there were some wonderful views. Rosamund (she had indicated very firmly to me that she did not like being called 'Rosie') became very excited. There was a shrubbery, and she led me down strange evergreen paths waving her arms in the air and saying, 'This is lovely! This is lovely!' She was leading me through a particularly dense mass of foliage when suddenly she stopped. 'The smell!' she said. 'What is it? It's delicious. Where is it coming from? It must be from one of these shrubs.' She dashed around sniffing. 'Just here. Stand here, Roland. Do you get it?'

Suddenly I smelt it. It was remarkably fragrant and sweet, but try as we might we could not find where it was coming from.

'I could die for that perfume, Roland.' She clutched my arm and buried her head against my chest, to my great embarrassment, and started breathing deeply. I could feel her breasts moving up and down against my body, which I really did not like. Then, slowly at first, she started to shake all over. Then her knees gave way and she slid down against my body and lay writhing on the ground in what appeared to be some sort of fit. I was horrified. I am hopeless when people are ill. I just feel sick and want to run away. But I remember being told once that you should put a pencil between an epileptic's teeth to stop them swallowing their tongue. I hadn't a pencil, but I reached for my fountain pen which was in my jacket pocket and slid it into her mouth. Her face, which had been ecstatic a few moments before, looked hideous. It was white and puffy and her eyeballs had rolled upwards. I realised I had to get help, so I ran to the house.

After what seemed like an hour, but was probably only seven or eight minutes, an ambulance came and I directed the men to where Rosamund lay. She seemed a little better. She opened her eyes and smiled but she was still shaking slightly. The men put her on a stretcher and I followed them back to the ambulance, asking them where they were taking her.

'A & E, mate,' was all I could get from them.

The ambulance drove off and then I realised that I was stranded! I don't carry a mobile phone and I hadn't even got a note of Margot's phone number with me. So I had to go to the tea room in the house and ask to use the phone and ring up directory enquiries to get her number and then phone her. She was appalled to hear what had happened and furious with me for not going with Rosamund in the ambulance.

'But I wasn't invited!' was all I could say.

When she'd calmed down, she said she'd come and pick me up and we'd both go to the local A & E Department, which was only five minutes away. I then raised the question of what was to happen to the car that Rosamund had borrowed and brought us in.

'For God's sake!!' was the only reply I got.

By the time we arrived at the hospital we were told that Ms Ehel (for that was Rosamund's name) was much better. They proposed to keep her in overnight for observation, but they would discharge her in the morning. Margot, who had been a nurse before she married, said she would pick her up and look after her.

I was sure that Rosamund had had an epileptic fit, but the following morning the hospital discharged her without comment and Margot insisted to me that it was 'just the time of the month' and that she'd probably been painting for too many hours at a stretch.

Margot loved being completely in charge of someone. She installed Rosamund in the bedroom next to mine and fed her hot Bovril and lightly boiled eggs. I was told to keep out of the way until the second morning, when I was told that Rosamund wanted to speak to me.

Margot stood to one side as I asked from the doorway, 'Are you feeling better?'

Rosamund held out her hand towards me and I gathered I was expected to go and hold it.

'The last thing I remember – and I shall always remember it – was you and me standing in the middle of that wonderful smell!'

'What was this?' said Margot sharply.

Rosamund continued, ignoring her, 'You're going to take me there again before it disappears. I want to stand there with you and enjoy it. Margot, would you take us this afternoon to the gardens?'

Margot of course would not hear of it.

'Ridiculous,' she said.

Rosamund pouted and then cried.

'Where is this place and what is this smell? Is it far from here?' snapped Margot.

'It's in the gardens,' I said. 'But Rosamund, do you really think you're better enough to be able to go?'

'Yes, yes, yes. Look, it was so strange and fugitive. If we wait even a day it may have gone for ever.'

'Now, Rosie,' said Margot in her best nurse's voice, 'just you listen to me. Roland, you'd better go to your room while I talk to her!'

I sighed inwardly and retired. I knew that when Margot was in this sort of mood there was no point in arguing. I didn't want to go back to the gardens myself. Something awful might happen again. I could hear the muffled sound of raised voices and crying from the next room. Eventually, after about five minutes, it died down and a few moments later there was a knock on my door. Margot appeared and said, 'I've agreed to take you both this afternoon provided you only stay for ten minutes.'

'I see,' I said.

'I'm not surprised you don't sound very enthusiastic. It's crazy if you ask me. But Rosie's become my best friend and she's in a terrible state and I suppose I must try and appease her.'

And so we all drove in Margot and Edwin's Jaguar (a relic from their Ealing days) up to the house and gardens immediately after lunch.

'You wait here please, Margot. I must go to this place alone with Roland.'

Margot raised her eyebrows and breathed heavily. 'Now you promise only to be away ten minutes. I'll be timing you. And Roland, you just look after her!'

So Rosamund and I set out for the shrubbery again. I glanced at her face and thought she looked very pale. She hadn't bothered to coil her hair and it was lying loosely on her shoulders. As we entered the shrubbery she said in a whisper, 'I'll go ahead. I'm glad there's no one else about. I wouldn't want to share it with anyone else. I think it was about here.'

She started sniffing the air.

I looked at her as she tiptoed in front of me. A strange little creature with wide shoulders and broad hips and chubby arms which were covered, like her face, in freckles.

'Just here, I think.'

She turned and took my hand and shut her eyes and breathed deeply.

'It's coming!' she whispered. 'There it is. Just a bit to the left.'

And there indeed was the same smell.

'Roland, please hold both my hands and face me.'

I complied awkwardly, feeling very foolish, and deeply regretted that I'd agreed to come.

'Roland, you've changed my life. I love you and we must get married.'

And then she literally hurled herself at me and flung her arms around me. Fortunately she was so short she couldn't reach my face otherwise I'm sure she would have kissed me. Even as it was I found it extremely unpleasant. Images of pushing my mother away when I was small when she tried to cuddle me and that awful girl at the college dance and, even worse, of Adam, my friend at university, pushing himself against me as I was bending over to tie my shoelace! I tried gently at first to push her away. It was no use. She clung to me desperately. She looked upwards from my shirt front and moaned, 'Kiss me, kiss me please, Roland. I can't bear this much longer!'

I tried even harder to push her away.

'You . . . can't be rejecting me! Roland, say something nice please.'

I said, 'Well, I like you of course, Rosamund. You're a very attractive girl with lovely hair, but I'm old enough to be your father.'

Images of what it would be like being married to Rosamund flashed through my brain. My ordered life in my flat would be disturbed. We'd have to buy a house with a studio for her and I should have to commute to work – oh, how awful!

Meanwhile, she'd become very still, but her arms were still locked around me. I'd given up trying to push her away.

'You've rejected me, haven't you? You've rejected me! I never thought you would be so cruel. I need you in order to paint well. If you turn me away I shall never paint again.'

It was so pathetic that I thought for a moment of saying something silly like, 'I'll think about it.' But I didn't. I could tell she was crying. And then, to my horror, she started to shake again just like she'd done before. And slowly her knees gave way and she slid down onto the ground. Last time she'd kept on shaking. This time her body gave three convulsive jerks and then she was still. She lay there on her back staring at the sky.

I raced off to find Margot. She was a nurse, she would know what to do.

'Oh dear, oh dear!' was all she said, then phoned for an ambulance on her mobile.

'Take me to her,' she said grimly.

When we got there Margot crouched down and felt Rosamund's temple.

'Oh God, she's dead! Poor little Rosie – my best friend. Why did she have to come here again?'

I stood there not knowing what to do or to think while my sister lay sobbing beside Rosamund's body.

When the paramedics arrived they tried to resuscitate her but gave up after a few minutes.

Margot's recriminations can be imagined! And it was even worse when Rosie's will was found. She'd left me everything!

I regret that I couldn't find any dealers who completely shared my enthusiasm for Rosamund's new work, but the pictures did all sell quite quickly for a few hundred each. But I've kept one. It hangs over the mantelpiece in my flat and I think it's very good. It's green, purple and mauve and the middle of it somehow disappears into the distance – I can't explain it better than that. Rosamund had written on the back the title of the picture. It was 'Seeking Paradise'.

Uncle Toby

I was feeling far from happy as I left the Underground at High Street Kensington and wheeled my suitcase behind me up the High Street and then into Campden Hill Road where my uncle Toby lived. It was late July four years ago and although only 9:30 it was already very, very warm. I thought of Eileen and our children, Freya and Joe, who would probably by now be on the beach in Norfolk, and wished I was there with them. But I didn't know then that my time with Uncle Toby was, for me, to be life changing!

'Well, hello my boy. Very glad to see you. You're looking well!'

Uncle Toby was bizarrely dressed in well-worn yellow cord trousers held up with an MCC tie around the waist, an open-necked white shirt, a bright green waistcoat and a blue blazer. He was propping himself up with a silver-handled walking stick and fanning his face with a Panama hat.

'Pretty warm isn't it?' he continued. 'Look, I'm all ready. My bag's in the car parked across the road – so let's go, shall we?'

Uncle Toby's car was a large and elderly Mercedes but I knew that it had air conditioning, and that was something to look forward to, I thought, as I put my case in the boot beside his somewhat battered leather suitcase.

'You know the way to get onto the M11 I'm sure,' he said,

'because I'd like a nap. Bit tiring having to do all my packing myself. Not used to it. No chauffeur, no housekeeper! A bit bereft! So grateful you could help out.'

With his silver-handled walking stick between his knees and his Panama over his eyes, Uncle Toby proceeded to go to sleep, snore gently and dribble slightly.

And so I negotiated the Mercedes through the London traffic and up the M11 and then the A11 to Norwich.

'Look, you've got to do it, Paul!' Eileen had said when the letter from Uncle Toby (or 'UT', as we knew him) arrived two weeks previously.

> *Dear Paul, I regret to tell you that I have not been at all well. And now at the same time my chauffeur who's been with me for ten years and my housekeeper who's been with me 25 have both come up for their retirement. I feel that at this stage in my life I may have to make other living arrangements. However, for the time being I am rather wanting to visit my old school and various other places of my foolish youth around Norwich and wonder if you, as my only close relative, would be prepared to drive me in the Merc and generally look after me. It will probably be the last opportunity I have as I'm a bit shaky on my pins! I know you teaching chaps have long holidays from mid-July onwards so maybe sometime within the next few weeks would be convenient for you. We shan't be away too long. Needless to say, I shall pay all expenses.*

'You *must* do it, Paul,' Eileen said very forcefully. 'It's a wonderful opportunity to make sure he leaves us his money.'

'But there's nobody else to leave it to.'

'You never know. Cats' homes and the like!'

'You know I planned to use this summer holiday trying to finish my PhD. Almost all the main writing is done. All I've got to do now is to put it in order. This will bugger my plans up completely!'

'No it won't. UT says you won't be away long!'

I had been working on my PhD thesis for a laughable twelve years. I'd started with good intentions, but the birth of two children and the dreadful consequences of having our house repossessed had put paid to them. It was easy to be wise later and see that we borrowed more than we could afford to repay if interest rates went up. But the bank had said that it would be okay, and we had Eileen's salary as she was still working then. However, as if it wasn't bad enough having the house repossessed, it had been sold by the Bank for £40,000 less than the amount we had borrowed and I was horrified when I was told that we would have to pay the £40,000 off by monthly instalments! That outgoing on top of the rent of the flat we had to move to in Battersea left hardly any spare money. Yes, so Eileen's point about inheriting from UT was very relevant. In fact, the thought of it had kept me going. UT had been a solicitor and then an MP and then the director of various companies and never married.

I really did want to finish my PhD but it was such hard work. I had started it with the idea that when I obtained it I could get a university post teaching history instead of displaying my historical knowledge to large classes of largely immigrant children at an inner London comprehensive. They had English as a second language and weren't very interested in history at all! And although I never consciously acknowledged it, I suppose the hope of UT's money must have contributed to my lack of progress with the PhD. With the inheritance I had visions of being able to buy another house and of being freed from the awful anxiety I constantly felt about not having enough money to pay for essentials.

As we drove into Norwich UT opened his eyes. Just under four hours it had taken us and we had had to stop in Newmarket as UT said he wanted to urinate! Arriving at the hotel, although he had slept most of the way, he announced that he was going to lie down and have a small meal sent up to his room. It did seem that he was not at all well! He suggested that I might like to have a late lunch somewhere and wander around Norwich, which I'd never been to before. It was not as hot as it had been in London and everything seemed very pleasant, particularly the area around the cathedral and its close, which was near to the hotel.

But by about five o'clock I thought I should be getting back. UT was in the entrance hall just finishing an animated conversation with the rather attractive blonde receptionist lady.

'Glad you liked the cathedral, my boy, I always thought it was very fine, even when I was at school. I'll give you a proper guided tour tomorrow morning. It is very instructive on the development of ecclesiastical architecture over several centuries as it took so long to build. Then in the afternoon, if I feel up to it, we'll have a look at the shops. Meet you in the bar at seven for a drink before dinner.'

Because I knew that UT had an almost pathological dislike of mobile phones, Eileen and I had agreed that I would not carry mine around with me, but if Eileen wanted anything urgently she would leave a message.

To say that Eileen was tense about life would be an understatement. To call her a drama queen would be incorrect because she didn't enjoy the frequent crises that we both seemed frequently to have to deal with at that time. So I was not surprised when I arrived in my bedroom and saw that there was a message from her on my mobile.

Help. Call ASAP. Eileen.

'What's the trouble?'

'Ah, thank God you've rung. Freya is ill. I think it's chicken pox. I can see one spot, but I'm not sure. I wanted to take her to the doctor we used last year when we were staying here but the car won't start. And I don't know the doctor's telephone number.'

'Oh dear. What's the matter with the car?'

'I told you – it won't start. It just splutters!'

'Well you'd better call the garage.'

'I don't know their phone number and I don't know their name. So I can't ask Directory Enquiries. Don't we belong to the AA or something?'

'I'm not sure. You'd better phone them. You'll be able to get their number from Directory Enquiries, and if we aren't members you'd better join.'

'I'm in a terrible state, Paul! I'm having diarrhoea.'

'Well take some Imodium.'

'I don't have any with me.'

'You can get some when you get the car started.'

'Yes, I suppose so. How are things with UT?'

'Fine, I think. Leave me another message to let me know how you get on.'

Although this was par for the course, every time Eileen had

one of her mini nervous breakdowns, as I'd come to think of them, I worried!

I slept badly that night. Throughout the tour of the cathedral the following morning, during which UT explained at great length the changes in the architectural style from Norman onwards as the building of the cathedral slowly progressed eastwards, my mind, although I pretended to be listening, was really focused on what might be happening to Eileen and the children. Particularly as I hadn't heard from her. Yes, goodness, UT's money would make a great difference. So many things can be solved quickly and easily if you can just use your credit card and not worry about it. The bungalow we had hired for the second year running at the coast was little more than a glorified beach hut. Several of the floorboards were rotten and there were cockroaches in the kitchen. But it was very, very cheap. How nice it would be to be able to stay in a really comfortable hotel!

But UT was now leading the way out of the door in the south transept of the cathedral so we could look at and admire the flying buttresses at the east end.

'And that's about it!' he said. 'Ah, forgot. Should have shown you the cloisters, but that's probably enough for one morning.'

So we made our way up the close and back into the city.

'It's nearly time for lunch. What I fancy is a Cromer crab and a pint of beer. How would that do you?'

'Very good, Uncle. But I thought you wanted to look at your old school.'

'Yes, well, I was talking to the receptionist in the hotel, as you saw, and she was telling me about the school now. Although the buildings haven't changed much, they don't take boarders any more. It's got about double the number of pupils it had in my day, and lots of them, God help me, are girls! It's totally changed. No point in looking!'

After finding a fish restaurant that had the desired crabs and beer, we consumed our meal and then UT proposed what he called a 'quick whizz' round the centre of the city. It was strange how his walking and general demeanour became much more spritely when he was obviously enjoying himself. But after looking at the market and his making some loud and derogatory comments about the architecture of the City Hall and the sartorial inelegance of the inhabitants, he announced that he was feeling tired, sat down on a bench and asked me to find him a taxi to drive us back to the hotel.

'And tomorrow,' he said in the taxi, 'I'd like you to drive me to Cromer where the crabs come from. That's where I learned to swim, you know.'

Please call was the message from Eileen when I got back to the hotel.

I tried to sound jovial as I spoke to her.

'How is it all going?'

I could feel the tension down the phone somehow.

'It's definitely chicken pox and I think Joe's got it too.'

'Oh dear! Did you see the doctor?'

'No. Once the car was repaired I went down to the village stores and they gave me the doctor's number. But when I rang the surgery, the doctor's receptionist said not to bring the kids there as they might be infectious. I eventually spoke to one of the doctors, a woman, but she didn't seem to want to visit us as we were only holidaymakers. She just said that I should put some calamine on the spots and both the children should get better. The spots are all in Freya's hair now and she keeps screaming all night because they're itching. And this morning there are five or six very naughty youths on motorbikes. They keep racing up and down the track over the dunes and making a terrible noise. I'm very frightened, Paul!'

'Well, do you want me to come?'

'No, no, no, no. You must stay. I just wanted to tell you.'

'Well, if it gets too bad, call the police.'

'Still going well?'

'Yes. Cathedral this morning and walk round the city this p.m. Tomorrow to Cromer.'

'Well, you won't be far away from us. Have a good time!'

'You know Cromer is either freezing cold or boiling hot. Generally the former!'

UT was right. The hot weather had suddenly given way to a grey sky and the temperature had plummeted. When we got to Cromer there was a sea mist which prevented UT from being able to point out the exact spot where he had managed his first strokes swimming in the sea.

'Of course, we didn't have heated swimming pools then. Everybody's getting soft these days.'

We had to look at the fishermen on the pier and I had to listen to reminiscences about summer shows at the pier pavilion and the launching of the lifeboat in rough seas. We then set off to walk round the town. This involved a pretty steep climb up a slipway by the moored crab boats. UT was panting with exertion when he suddenly stopped in front of a shop which said in large gilt letters across its window 'Unisex hairdresser'.

Behind the lettering a young blonde lady, obviously of Eastern European origin, was cutting an elderly lady's hair.

'Just look at that hairdresser girl! Isn't she a stunner? … Er … I'm going to have a haircut this afternoon I think. You just stay there.'

And so saying, UT proceeded majestically into the shop, the bell on the door making a loud clanging as he did so.

I knew that in his younger days UT had had a certain reputation with the ladies, and can remember reading about him in the gossip columns. But that must have been years and years and years ago!

'Yes, I've made an appointment for three o'clock,' he said returning and grinning. 'So let's go and get something to eat now so that I shan't be late.'

As I ate another crab and surveyed my uncle's hair I came to the conclusion that it really didn't need cutting.

While UT had his hair cut I walked on the beach watching people trying, rather unsuccessfully, to surf. The sun had come out and, as UT predicted, Cromer suddenly became very hot! I met him again as arranged at quarter to four by the church. He took off his hat.

'What do you think?' he asked.

I thought his hair looked roughly the same as before, but it smelled strongly of something that had obviously been sprayed on it.

'What a lovely girl, Paul. Cut it very carefully. So nice and friendly. It may surprise you, but I've asked her out to dinner tonight.'

'Oh, where?'

'There are several places along the coast road she said. I'm sure we'll get in somewhere.'

He was in a very good mood on the drive back to Norwich and kept up a constant stream of conversation.

'All these dreadful little bungalows that are springing up everywhere. Don't know how people can live in them – absolutely soulless!'

'Well, they just want somewhere to live; that's all,' I replied.

'I know. A nice little bungalow bought with a mortgage and a little Ford or Vauxhall in the drive on hire purchase or whatever they call it nowadays. Did you notice those candles burning in Norwich Cathedral? Votive candles they're called I believe – sort of in place of a prayer. You put 50p in the box and light a candle and that's instead of praying. Funny business. It was called a Popish practice when I was young and certainly they wouldn't have had it in the cathedral. Just shows. The Church of England simply does not know what it's doing or where it's going. Always did try to please everyone, of course, a bit like the Liberal Democrats. Agniezka, she's called, the hairdresser. Polish of course. Been here a couple of years. Likes it. Her English is quite good although I was a bit puzzled by some of the things she tried to explain.

'Ah, here we are. I'll have a short rest before we set off. Better start at six thirty to be on the safe side. Now I hope you don't mind, but I'll do this dinner on my own. You just drop us and I'm sure you'll find somewhere nearby to eat and spend the evening. If you give me your mobile number I'll phone you when we are ready to be picked up.'

*

'Eileen, it's me. How is everything? … This is my first opportunity … You've been on the beach? Good – in spite of the chicken pox! … Well, the weather got better, didn't it, in the afternoon. … And the motorcyclists have gone? I see, somebody called the police. Good. … Yes, it was quite nice in Cromer and it got quite hot after the mist cleared. But do you know the old boy's picked up a young Polish hairdresser and is taking her out to dinner this evening? I don't know if it's serious. … Well, what can I do about it? … Yes, she's a nice-looking girl from what I've seen of her. About thirty I should have thought. … I agree, we don't want him getting married in his dotage. … Yes, he's at an awkward age, I know. … No, I don't think she looks too predatory – just after a free meal at a good restaurant maybe. … Look, calm down! The children must be feeling better if they're on the beach. I'll ring you later this evening when we get back to the hotel, so keep your phone switched on.'

I was despatched by UT to the nearest flower stall to get a really big bunch of roses before we set off gain for Cromer.

Agniezka lived in a dull little house in a side street, no doubt inhabited by several other Poles. I hoped she had a boyfriend! I was instructed to go to the front door, knock on it, then present the roses and say: 'From Toby. He's waiting in the car.'

Agniezka sat on the back seat of the car with UT. I took surreptitious glances at her in the rear-view mirror when I could as we drove along the coast road. Yes, she had got herself up a bit and looked very pretty. Uncle Toby was sitting very close to her and talking to her in such low tones that I couldn't hear what he was saying. They managed to get a table at the first restaurant we stopped at. It looked very expensive! And I spent a very boring evening in the nearest pub I could find.

At last, just after ten thirty, my mobile rang.

'Paul, will you come and pick me up as soon as possible.'

He didn't sound at all happy.

'From the restaurant?'

'No, I'll be sitting in the bus shelter opposite. I want a breath of fresh air.'

I managed to get to the bus shelter in just under five minutes. There was a street lamp nearby and I could see Uncle Toby huddled in the corner. He was alone. He didn't move as the car pulled up. I got out and went over to him. To my amazement he was crying. The tears were trickling down his mottled cheeks and I noticed that he had a bruise under his right eye.

'What on earth is the matter, Uncle? Where is Agniezka?'

Uncle Toby rallied a little and forced a bit of a smile.

'She went home on the bus.'

'Oh. What went wrong?'

'I don't really want to talk about it, but you'd better know that she said I was a silly old fool and hit me. Have I got a black eye?'

'Well, a bit of one.'

'Let's go back to Norwich.'

UT's smart suit that he had put on for the occasion looked distinctly sad and crumpled as he sat beside me in the front of the car. He'd stopped weeping, and was totally silent except for snuffling from time to time. Eventually, he took a deep breath and made a long speech, looking straight ahead at the road.

'You probably thought it was very odd my asking that young woman out to dinner, but there was a reason. If I may digress – it's true that my housekeeper retired – she was seventy – but I sacked my chauffeur as, frankly, I couldn't afford him any more. In reality, I could hardly afford the housekeeper either. You see, at one time I was quite well off, but then there was all that wretched business with Lloyd's Names. I was one of the "names" of course and lost a packet. Nearly broke me, but I had the house and you can take out things called equity releases. Gives you capital which is repaid out of the sale of the house when you die. So I took out quite a large sum by this equity release business as the house had gone up hugely in value since I'd bought it. My financial advisor (curse them all!) told me to put the money into one of these hedge-fund things. Of course, the hedge fund did terribly badly, but with the income that I can still get from it and my state pension I've just about enough to live on. I'll have to sell the car. It guzzles petrol. But I'm a bit tottery as you can see and need looking after. I've been thinking about it a lot and when I saw that girl in that hairdresser's, obviously an Eastern European girl, I thought she might be interested in, well … you know, coming to live in my house rent free and doing a bit of housekeeping as well as hairdressing. I've got a friend who's managed a similar arrangement. These immigrant girls are often wanting something like that. Well, I picked the wrong one. I admit I did put my hand on her knee under the table, which was silly of me, but she was awfully attractive and I thought she might like it. But she didn't. She caused an awful scene in the restaurant and stormed off to catch the bus. She must have known that one was coming at that time. I went to the bus shelter and pleaded with her, but it was no good. That was when she called me a silly old fool and hit me. I had to cover my face with a handkerchief and go back into the restaurant to call you on the telephone.

'So I don't know what I'm going to do now. I had hoped, you know, Paul, that I'd be able to leave you quite a bit because you've got a neurotic wife and two children and have had a very bad time financially. But there we are. You know it all now!'

And so vanished the fantasy of inheriting Uncle Toby's money; instead I had to accept the reality of having to finish my PhD, which I did quite quickly. But it took much longer to get a post at a university.

What happened to Uncle Toby is another story.

Day Trip to Manly

Somebody once said that the one good thing about spending February in Britain was that it only lasted 28 days.

By mid-January I couldn't bear the prospect of the gloom. Sunshine beckoned; but was it to be the West Indies, South Africa or Australia? Even though it's a long flight, Australia won, mainly because my wife had died and I didn't like having holidays on my own, and I had some cousins in Sydney who seemed delighted at the thought of my staying with them.

It was a mistake, I realised, after the third day, and so I think did they. Day 1, I rested, day 2, they showed me some sights, day 3, cousin Annie (she was only 50) complained that her legs hurt and Bill had an asthma attack!

'You'd better go off on your own today. Why don't you take the boat to Manly? You'll like it there.'

And it did seem a very nice place, although I don't remember it in much detail. But the sun was shining and I found the beach. The waves were breaking, the surfers were surfing and I was wandering along in my shirt, shorts and sandals, very conscious of my elderly white knobbly legs. I was trying to think of a gentle way of detaching myself from my cousins – a trip to Brisbane perhaps? – when what looked like a child's exercise book came blowing along the pavement towards me in the wind. I felt I couldn't just let it blow away, so, as bending had become a bit of a problem, I put my foot on the book and then gently bent to pick it up. Unfortunately, I'd left a dirty print of the sole of my sandal on the cover. I opened it up. On the first page in big block capitals was written: 'I HOPE NOBODY EVER READS THIS'.

Of course, I promptly sat down on the nearest seat, turned the page and started reading. The writing was obviously not a child's. It was rather good, in an old-fashioned style – somewhat like my own; the sort of thing they taught you in school in England during and just after the war. I read:

I was a newly qualified solicitor working in London. Things in the 1950s were very different from today. Now, solicitors' offices are quite smart and some even have air conditioning. The firm I worked for had its offices in Holborn: Bedford Row. There were only two partners (that was quite usual then), three managing clerks, two lady secretaries, a telephonist/receptionist, a junior clerk/office boy, and me. The partners had a good room each on the first floor of what originally had been a rather fine Georgian house, with their secretaries in an office together near them. The ground floor had been badly and cheaply partitioned to form a reception area, where the telephonist sat, a waiting room and two cubby holes for two of the managing clerks. In the basement was the other managing clerk, file storage and a strong room. I was on the top floor in a small room which overlooked a dismal back yard. The rest of the top floor was let out to a Chartered Patent Agent. He never seemed to be there. I'm sure my room had not been painted since before the 1939-45 war. There was cracked lino on the floor and a square of worn red carpet under my dilapidated desk and chair. I had a telephone and an unreliable dictating machine. The fireplace had been blocked up and heat was provided by a one-bar electric fire which was totally inadequate in winter, so when it was cold I had to come to work in a thick suit and a pullover. In a corner of the room by the door was a photocopying machine which everyone (apart from the partners) came and used from time to time. It was a ghastly contraption which had to be filled with smelly liquid chemicals. I forget exactly how it worked but each page took some time to copy. I resented the presence of the machine greatly, particularly if it was being used while I was trying to interview a client. Not that my work was very important. It consisted mainly of house purchasing, disputes between neighbours, minor road accidents, and landlord and tenant problems. The partners treated me with formality and a certain amount of what I regarded as contempt and the managing clerks as 'not one of them', because I was qualified. The secretaries (both of uncertain age) seemed to have a conspiracy to 'keep me in my place' – wherever that was supposed to be. They condescended to type my work 'if they were not too busy'. So I was not very happy at work and it was even worse at home.

I had married Audrey eighteen months previously. The first problem was with her parents. They were very comfortably off, but when I talked to Audrey's father about getting married (you did that in those days) he stipulated that I should buy her a house and be able to support her financially otherwise he would be opposed to the idea. I'm not quite sure what he would have done if I hadn't agreed. But I invested all the money my father had left me (and which I had been living on while I was an articled clerk) into a semi-detached house in East Finchley. Having then only my meagre salary, we had little spare money and I had to redecorate the inside of the house myself. Not something I enjoyed! Audrey had given up her job as a teacher before we got married. No doubt her father told her it was unseemly for married women to work. She quickly became bored and discontented and continued to be like that even after I had slaved for many evenings and weekends redecorating every room in the house. Then she became pregnant and that's when the troubles really started. I'm not sure how ill she really felt, but she moaned all day and half the night about feeling sick, having heartburn, putting on weight, etc., etc. To me, she became physically very unattractive. I almost dreaded coming home from the office.

And then the baby was born – a boy. I think Audrey must have been a bad mother because he cried all night, every night – at least that's how I remember it! She was constantly rushing him to the doctor with some ailment or other; largely imaginary I suspected. At first, she kept giving me the baby, Andrew, to hold, but after a few weeks she said I was 'hopeless' with him and wouldn't let me touch him. She said I 'upset him'. So things progressed from bad to worse. It was when he started to crawl I think that Andrew began to hate me. I remember one day when his mother was out of the room, I knelt down beside him and made the silly animal noises that babies are supposed to like. But Andrew just gazed at me with an expression of such malevolence that I was almost frightened. And then he let out the most terrible howling noise so that Audrey came rushing from the kitchen and saw me with him on the floor.

'What are you doing to him?' she shouted. 'Leave him alone!'

From then on things were never the same between us.

And then things at work became unpleasant.

One morning I was summoned into one of the partner's offices – Mr Budgen (name changed). I remember him well. Three-piece suit, watch chain, moustache, pompous manner. His verbal delivery was very similar to Mr Macmillan's, the Prime Minister of the time.

'Well, Smithers (again name changed),' he said, 'I wanted to have a word with you. We're taking on a junior partner with a connection

of his own. We shall need your room to accommodate him. So from next Monday you'll have to move to the basement and share with Mills. Sorry about that, but it can't be helped. I'll speak to Mills in due course. I think there's a spare table in his room.'

I visualised Mills's room. There was indeed a side table piled high with old files. The table was also home to the kettle and tea things for making drinks for the whole firm! Mills was very grumpy and elderly and smelt of mothballs. I had no doubt that he would be about as pleased with the arrangement as I was.

'What about when I see clients, sir?' was the only reply I gave.

'You'll have to manage that as well as you can, I'm afraid.'

I think today it would be called 'constructive dismissal'. During my lunch hour I went to the Law Society in Chancery Lane and looked at their Appointments Vacant list, but there didn't seem to be anything suitable for me. I'd have to wait until the advertisements appeared in the next issue of the Gazette. I think I must have been very angry.

And it was the same day that when I arrived home I found Audrey sitting red-faced on the sofa and crying. There was no sign of Andrew and at first I thought he must be ill or even have died.

'What is the matter?' I asked.

'Auntie Gladys is dead.'

'Oh. Where's Andrew?'

'He's cried himself to sleep. He's very upset, too.'

How a small baby could be so upset about the death of a relative whom he had probably only seen two or three times was a mystery to me, but I said nothing.

I had only met Auntie Gladys twice and we had taken an instant dislike to one another. Gladys was Audrey's mother's unmarried sister.

She lived in a small house near Richmond crammed with antiques and knick-knacks.

'She's very wealthy,' Audrey had whispered to me as we went to see her shortly after our engagement, 'and she says she's going to leave everything to me. So be nice to her.'

Well, she had left everything to Audrey, who for a few days cheered up considerably at the thought.

'I hope your firm will do the probate work for free,' she said.

I very much doubted that, but I thought they might do it at a concessionary rate.

'We'll give your wife a ten per cent reduction on the scale,' said Mr Budgen, 'as you tell me you think it's quite a substantial estate. Norman had better go with you to take the inventory.'

I should explain that Audrey had already indicated that she was far too busy looking after Andrew and wanted me to deal with the house contents. So a few days after the funeral, which was a very tearful affair on the part of Audrey and her mother, I duly went by train to Richmond with Norman and then by taxi to Gladys's house. Norman, the firm's probate clerk, was called by his Christian name because he'd worked his way up from being the office boy. He was sharp-suited, cheeky and brash. I always thought he had a secret ambition to get himself qualified as a solicitor.

'Bloody lucky you are, James. Your wife's going to be rich. Be able to set up in practice on your own no doubt. Can't be much fun for you down in the basement with old Mills. You're starting to smell of mothballs yourself, I think,' he said, sniffing loudly.

In fact old Mills had made me quite welcome in his grumpy way. We'd moved the tea things and files off his side table and he'd put the telephone on the side of his desk so that I could reach it if a call came through for me.

'I don't think they like either of us very much, young Jim,' he'd said. 'Still, you can always move on. I'm stuck here until I retire. It's because of my pension, you see.' (You couldn't easily 'move' pensions in those days.)

I must have been thinking about 'moving on' when we arrived at the house. Norman was still blithering on about how I'd be able to start a new practice. I couldn't imagine Audrey in her present frame of mind giving me anything. In fact, she'd probably want to take Andrew and go and live somewhere on her own. As we went through Auntie Gladys's front door, Norman said, 'You know the reason why I've had to bloody come with you? Old Budgen wanted me to keep an eye on you to make sure you didn't pocket any nice pieces of jewellery!'

At that moment a sort of red haze of rage appeared about two or three feet in front of my eyes. 'The miserable old bugger,' I thought. It was a totally unwarranted defamatory remark about an employee who'd never shown any signs of dishonesty. Why was everyone against me? My wife didn't like me, my son seemed to hate me. Although I'd done exactly as they wanted, my wife's parents seemed to despise me and this idiot Norman obviously thought it was funny that I should be thought of as a potential thief. Whether at that moment I resolved to steal something I'm not sure, although I think it was at that moment that I remembered that Audrey had said to me:

'Look inside Auntie's desk won't you? She always hinted that there was a secret drawer or compartment or something. So it may have something valuable in it!'

Norman had made straight for the desk which was in the living room. Well, the desk was in fact a large bureau with a pull-down front, which he opened, causing a shower of share certificates to fall out all over the floor, much to his glee.

'Look at that, Jim. God, she must have been rolling in it.'

He gathered them all up and took them over to the dining table.

'Look at that, 20,000 Imps, 10,000 ICI, for a start. Have a look and see if there's a valuation from her brokers anywhere. It'll make things a bit easier if we can make sure we've got all the certificates.'

But first I foraged about in the bureau, remembering Audrey's words about the secret drawer. It was easy! I'd seen the sort of thing before. I pressed down on one of the compartments and what looked like a blank piece of wood clicked out about an inch. Obscuring Norman's view from where he was sitting at the table gloating over the share certificates, I slid the drawer out a little further and put my hand inside. There was a stone there, the size of a large pebble. I picked it up, slid it into my jacket pocket and shut the drawer. Then I pulled a chair up to the desk and started to sort systematically through its contents.

I knew nothing about diamonds or their value. But that's undoubtedly what the stone was. I can't remember the exact moment when I decided to keep it. At first, I felt very nervous. I didn't know where to hide the thing. I kept moving it around; first in one pocket and then in another. Often I walked around the streets of Holborn 'wrestling with my conscience', I think it's called. I was miserable in the basement. They'd stopped giving me any new work to do. They were presumably giving it to the new partner. He didn't seem a bad sort of chap. A bit haughty, but not unkind. Obviously they wanted me to leave. At home Andrew had become totally and unhealthily attached to Audrey. He cried if she disappeared from his sight, even to go to the bathroom. So she took him with her wherever she went and even started sleeping in a small bed in his room. Andrew was her child and I had no part in his life, nor, it seemed, in hers.

I half expected that Gladys had left a note or something mentioning the diamond. If such a note turned up I resolved that I would feign ignorance of the secret drawer but go and investigate and find the drawer empty. Anyone could have taken the stone or Gladys could have given it away. But no note about the diamond emerged from the piles of paper. Even without the diamond, I could see Audrey would now be worth a small fortune – but that didn't concern me, for I had the diamond!

Four weeks after Gladys's death, I disappeared from East Finchley and Holborn and, like Mr Stonehouse some years later, wound up here in Australia. That was the easy bit. I felt no guilt at leaving the firm or my wife and son. Audrey would in due course no doubt claim the house that I'd paid for and get the money from my life insurance. Turning the diamond into cash was the difficult bit . . .

At that moment there was a shout of rage and the exercise book was wrenched from my hands.

'You're not to read it. It's mine!'

It was taken with such force that I lost my balance and fell off the seat. As I sprawled on the ground, I turned my head to see a grey-haired and bearded figure in jeans and a T-shirt with a butcher's apron tied over them running away across the street, clutching the exercise book to his chest. He then disappeared into one of the restaurants that lined the seafront.

As I sat up trying to recover my composure, a young man – a typically bronzed young Australian – came and helped me up.

'Don't worry, mate, he's really quite harmless, although he gets excited at times. A bit off his head. Washes up in the restaurant over there. You okay?'

'I think so,' I said. 'Thank you.'

But it had spoiled my trip to Manly. Not only was I shaken up by my fall, I was disturbed by the story in the exercise book. I knew the details were totally exact for the period as I'd been practising as a solicitor in London myself in the 1950s. As I stood by the rail on the return boat and looked back at the wake it was making, I thought about the past.

I had briefly become a partner at that time in a firm in Bedford Row, displacing a young solicitor from his office. He'd been very resentful, and then I heard that he had disappeared. I wondered . . . it seemed so unlikely!